Something had blown the Executioner's sleep apart

Bolan rolled off the bed, grabbing the Desert Eagle on the way. He rose into a crouch, the big .44 Magnum already leveled toward the door.

He reached for Ramona, meaning to jerk her off the bed to the floor, but then as a long-honed sense had told him would happen, the door erupted in an explosion of wood, bits and pieces flying ahead of a burst of heavy slugs.

The gunner had aimed a little high, the stream of steel chopping the wall just above Ramona. The Executioner fired just once, through the hole already blown through the wooden door. A quick burst drilled into the ceiling, the last reflexive act of a dying man.

Terrified, Ramona sat up.

"Down!" Bolan yelled.

She was quick, rolling off the bed on the opposite side just as a second stream of slugs thudded into the mattress....

MACK BOLAN®

The Executioner

DON PENDLETON'S
THE EXECUTIONER®
FEATURING MACK BOLAN®

FIREBASE FLORIDA

A GOLD EAGLE BOOK FROM
WORLDWIDE®

TORONTO • NEW YORK • LONDON • PARIS
AMSTERDAM • STOCKHOLM • HAMBURG
ATHENS • MILAN • TOKYO • SYDNEY

First edition September 1991

ISBN 0-373-61153-6

Special thanks and acknowledgment to
Carl Furst for his contribution to this work.

FIREBASE FLORIDA

Printed in U.S.A.

The superior man . . . is eyes for the blind, strength for the weak, and a shield for the defenseless. He stands erect by bending above the fallen. He rises by lifting others.

—Robert Green Ingersoll
1833–1899

They are slaves who fear to speak for the fallen and the weak.

—James Russell Lowell
1819–1891

Predators prey upon the weak, against those powerless to fight back. I'll stand at their defense until they can fight their own battles—and win.

—Mack Bolan

THE
MACK BOLAN®
LEGEND

Nothing less than a war could have fashioned the destiny of the man called Mack Bolan. Bolan earned the Executioner title in the jungle hell of Vietnam.

But this soldier also wore another name—Sergeant Mercy. He was so tagged because of the compassion he showed to wounded comrades-in-arms and Vietnamese civilians.

Mack Bolan's second tour of duty ended prematurely when he was given emergency leave to return home and bury his family, victims of the Mob. Then he declared a one-man war against the Mafia.

He confronted the Families head-on from coast to coast, and soon a hope of victory began to appear. But Bolan had broken society's every rule. That same society started gunning for this elusive warrior—to no avail.

So Bolan was offered amnesty to work within the system against terrorism. This time, as an employee of Uncle Sam, Bolan became Colonel John Phoenix. With a command center at Stony Man Farm in Virginia, he and his new allies—Able Team and Phoenix Force—waged relentless war on a new adversary: the KGB.

But when his one true love, April Rose, died at the hands of the Soviet terror machine, Bolan severed all ties with Establishment authority.

Now, after a lengthy lone-wolf struggle and much soul-searching, the Executioner has agreed to enter an ''arm's-length'' alliance with his government once more, reserving the right to pursue personal missions in his Everlasting War.

1

Mack Bolan sat in the passenger seat, glancing alertly back and forth between the driver and the dark urban streets through which they were moving. The car was air-conditioned, but the worn-out machinery labored without complete success against the oppressive heat and humidity of the tropical night.

Miami. The Executioner had fought here many times before. The friendly ghosts were everywhere.

The man who was driving the car was an old acquaintance. It was strange how things worked out. Jorge Iturbe was a detective sergeant now, of the Miami police. The car they were traveling in was an unmarked police car. Iturbe had turned the volume down low on the police radio, but the voices still came through: laconic, mechanical, a steady stream of communication. A man could train himself to ignore unbroken radio chatter, seeming hardly to hear it at all, yet alert to a few words and phrases that would focus all his attention in an instant.

Jorge Iturbe drew smoke from a small, thin cigar. He was, as he had always been, a slender man with a knife-sharp face: long, pointed jaw, thin nose. In the old days he'd been wiry, a man with muscles like steel cables, who could swim two miles without showing need for breath, then climb a cliff face and scramble out at the top, weapons ready, determined and deadly. He'd been a warrior.

Hell, he was still a warrior, Bolan decided. But different. He'd remained basically thin and still had that knife-sharp face, but the muscles had grown a little slack, the waist a little thick.

"For twenty years," Jorge said, "I kept the cubano dream alive."

"The dream of going home," Bolan stated.

Iturbe nodded. "Back to Cuba. I used to dream of firing the shots that would eliminate that murderous bastard Castro. I mean, that was the dream, comandante—of putting a stream of 9 mm slugs into his belly."

He called Bolan "comandante" because the Executioner had once led a team of Cubans on a raid against a gang of Cuban Reds who had slaughtered a group of innocent Cuban patriots.

"Sometimes it's impossible to keep the dream alive, I suppose," Bolan commented.

"Ah, but *you* have. You never gave up, did you? I mean, you're still trying to make this world a better place."

Bolan could hear the respect in the man's voice and knew that to some extent Jorge Iturbe was conceding that he had, to one degree or another, surrendered. Or, more accurately stated, Jorge had made his peace with the world.

In a way the warrior never had, never could.

"I got married, comandante," Iturbe said. "That makes a difference, you know. I have two little girls at home. And you know what? I'm a citizen of the United States now.''

"You're still fighting the war, Jorge," Bolan told him. "I can think of a hundred ways you could make a living, a good living—a man with your talents. You didn't become a policeman because you backed away from the good fight."

Iturbe glanced at the hard face that hadn't changed much in the years since they'd fought side by side. The man—Iturbe didn't know his name; comandante was good enough—was still the man he'd been before: strong, solemn, committed and unswerving. And generally silent. Observing. Intense. A man who didn't make compromises.

"Things haven't changed."

"That's the word I got," Bolan replied.

"They don't fight exactly the same way anymore. They don't fight tougher, but they fight meaner. Dirtier."

"So I hear."

"You remember the phrase 'the best and the brightest'?" Jorge asked. "Well, the best and the brightest pulled out of Fidel's Cuba. They came to Florida, because it was the closest place across the water. And we've done damn well, you know."

"You've elected a mayor."

"Mayor of Miami, right," Iturbe agreed. "But there's more to it than that. We— Hold it."

He'd caught something on the radio.

"Oh, shit." Iturbe stomped on the accelerator, rolled down the window, slammed a flashing red emergency light on top of the car—where it stuck with a strong magnet—and activated a wailing siren.

"What have you got, Jorge?" Bolan asked. He'd already unleathered his .44 Desert Eagle, the big, powerful automatic he'd come to favor. "Trouble?"

"The code," Jorge said tensely. "'Come to the assistance of officers in trouble. Proceed with caution.' It's in the fan."

Suddenly the married man and father of two was the old Jorge, the fighter. Bolan jerked on his seat belt to tighten it as Iturbe sent the aging Chevrolet hurtling through dark and dimly lighted streets. Siren blaring, horn honking, lights blinking, he plunged into the traffic in intersections, driving through narrow gaps between moving cars and trucks. He accelerated to fifty miles an hour, then to sixty.

Bolan knew the streets of Miami well enough to know they were traveling due west through neighborhoods that didn't look too good. He was listening closely to the radio now.

"All units alert. Coral South and Thirty-first. Officers under fire."

"Damn!" Jorge yelled.

"Any ideas?" Bolan asked.

The detective glanced at him, his eyes white and wild. "Cubano neighborhood," he muttered. "Cubano cops."

And that proved to be true. Their car was the third to arrive to help the officers in unit 282. The vehicle was stopped in the intersection of Coral South and Thirty-first, its front tires flat and its front fenders peppered with shotgun fire.

Three police cars. Now four. But whoever had shot out the tires of unit 282 hadn't retreated. Firing continued.

"Comandante!" Iturbe shouted as Bolan rolled out the right door. "Wait here!"

The detective reached into the back seat, grabbed a Miami police baseball cap and an orange vest emblazoned with MPD and handed them to Bolan.

"Our guys will shoot—"

"Understood," Bolan barked impatiently. He jammed the cap onto his head and shrugged into the vest. "Over there!"

The warrior, long experienced in spotting a sniper's nest, had located a blue-yellow muzzle-flash. Crouching low, he trotted toward the flash of light. A burst of automatic gunfire blasted through the Chevrolet he and the detective had just left.

Another police unit sped into the intersection—to be met with a heavy blast from the gun Bolan had first spotted. He guessed the weapon was a big shotgun, spewing out a storm of heavy pellets.

Then a second blast took out the windshield, which located the shotgunner for the Executioner. He leveled the Desert Eagle and fired one .44 Magnum round.

The flash lit the porch where the shotgunner had been hiding and firing, just long enough to let anyone who was watching see the gunner's chest explode under the impact of the big high-velocity slug.

The muzzle-flash from the Desert Eagle was immediately the target for half a dozen shots. Bolan had known it would be and had thrown himself to the left and to the pavement.

The man firing the automatic had made himself a target by the sustained flash from his stream of fire. He was the tough one, the one Bolan wanted next—the man with the assault gun.

A cop made himself the target that let Bolan pinpoint the guy. Running for a better place—better to see, better to shoot—a cop, probably a young fellow, took the fury of a blast from whatever the guy with the assault gun was firing.

That muzzle-flash was what the Executioner needed. He aimed and fired, but the guy had moved.

The gunner saw the muzzle-flash of the .44 Magnum and swung his assault gun around to get off a shot. Bolan, in another position, was watching for the muzzle-flash. He saw it. A blast from the Desert Eagle threw the gunman off his feet, slamming him back against a brick wall.

The Executioner looked back at the police car that had originally called for help. It had been totaled, hit by heavy blasts from one or more short-barreled shotguns and by automatic fire from 9 mm automatics.

One of the officers was dead. For sure. The other… Bolan didn't see him. Maybe the other officer had gotten out.

Police cars sped into the intersection. A dozen of them in a few minutes.

Bolan went looking for Jorge Iturbe.

"This is the way it goes," Iturbe told him. "I wanted you to see. Now we can talk, and you won't think I'm exaggerating."

"I'd never think that, Jorge. I know you better than that. Trust you more than that."

They stood in the middle of the intersection. Cops spread out now in combat gear, working more like infantrymen than policemen. A couple of shots were fired at them from snipers, then it was over. It was quiet.

Iturbe handed Bolan's police cap and vest to a uniformed sergeant. "Unofficial help," he said to the man. "No questions asked, okay?"

The sergeant nodded, then frowned as the detective and Bolan walked away, as if the big warrior reminded him of someone.

The Miami police had suffered one man killed—the young officer slumped behind the shattered windshield of car 282. They had three wounded, one seriously.

The attackers had two dead—both blown apart by 44 Magnum slugs. One guy's legs had been shattered by buckshot from a police shotgun. The rest had escaped, wounded or not.

Ambulances screamed into the intersection, followed two minutes later by the first camera van from a television station.

Jorge Iturbe jerked his head, signaling Bolan to follow him. He walked purposefully along Coral Street South—out of the picture the camera van would shortly be transmitting.

"I don't want them to get a picture of you, comandante. The young officer who was killed in the first car was named Ricardo Galvez. Cubano. His partner was another cubano. The reinforcements were mostly

Anglo. Galvez is the fifth cubano officer killed this year."

"Why?" Bolan asked. "What are they doing?"

"Frightening people," Iturbe replied. "Terrorism."

"Okay. So who's doing it and why?"

"Two kinds of people are doing it, as near as I can figure out."

The detective had slowed his pace, and they were walking almost casually along a street of small shops, mostly closed at this hour. A couple of bars were open. They walked by a newsstand selling Spanish-language newspapers and magazines. There were homes on the street, too, and people strolling and chatting.

"Two kinds," Iturbe continued. "In the first place, just crooks. The kind of scum the human race seems to produce, anytime, anywhere. I don't need to tell you. But the other kind are hard-line, unrepentant Communists. Marxists, Leninists, Fidelistos..."

He led Bolan through the open double doors of one of the bars. It was a cantina, the kind Bolan had seen in countries all over Central and South America. It was crowded. Every table was taken, and people stood around in groups, talking and sipping wine or beer. At the far end of the big, smoky room two men played guitars and a few young people were dancing. The atmosphere was close and hot, and to the smell of smoke, wine and beer was added the stench of sweat.

Iturbe bought a large glass of red wine for himself and a bottle of cold beer for Bolan.

"We'll meet two or three friends of mine here maybe."

Bolan nodded. "You were starting to tell me why..."

"Right. Okay, in a few words, most cubanos came to Florida very poor, refugees from Fidel, with nothing but the clothes on their backs. I myself was brought by my father and mother, and I can tell you they came with nothing but what they were wearing. Today my father owns a real-estate agency. He drives a Mercedes. And he's typical. Cubanos own banks, automobile agencies, factories, stores. My father and mother have long since given up the idea that they'll ever go back to Cuba. The generation who was born here—and that's all the young people—couldn't be dragged back."

"There was a time when you would have gone, Jorge," Bolan reminded him.

The detective nodded. "As a soldier. There are still those who dream of that, including a few of the young people. Anyway, we're a prosperous community, and we're a varied community. Which means that we include the despicable criminals I've mentioned. It also means that in our midst we have some of the Red fanatics I've also mentioned. And they mean to prey on us. Both kinds of them. They've formed an alliance."

"To do what?" Bolan asked.

"Loot the community, the same way the Five Families loot New York. A cubano Mafia. They deal in drugs, of course, but, well, if they didn't somebody else would, so that's not the worst they do. They sell 'protection.' Constant, organized extortion. They trap young girls into prostitution. They've taken over certain kinds of businesses, just like the Mafia does. Services. You know the routine. Plus, they're heavily into weapons. Central and South America is a big market for infantry weapons."

"Why the attacks on the police?"

"They want the cubano community to know who's boss. They want to make it appear the police can't protect anybody."

"So the point is to fight back?"

"That's why you're here, comandante. We hope you'll take up the good fight."

"Are your people willing to fight?" Bolan asked.

"Yes. Some are."

"All it takes is 'some.' That's all it ever takes—a few good men."

"We have them," Iturbe promised. "You'll see. We have a few good men. More than a few."

2

By the time they left the cantina half an hour later, two of Iturbe's "good men" had shown up.

Tomás Urbina was a hard-faced, hard-muscled young man. His dark brown eyes met Bolan's without flinching.

The second man was Homero Alvarado, and he was very unlike Tomás Urbina. Alvarado was gracefully thin in contrast to the solid Urbina. His eyes met Bolan's, but quickly flicked around, checking out everything and everyone in the cantina. He was nervously alert.

They didn't talk long. As Iturbe had said, both these younger men had heard of El Comandante, but both had been reluctant to believe the stories were of a real man. Urbina accepted the detective's word that this was the famous warrior who had helped the cubanos win important battles some years ago. Alvarado reserved judgment.

In any case, none of them were men of many words. The two new arrivals had something to show the Executioner, something Iturbe wanted him to see; and shortly they left the cantina and drove away in a huge old Cadillac convertible.

They passed within a block of the intersection where
the shoot-out had occurred. The streets were still
jammed with vehicles: police cars, emergency squad
wagons and news vans. Cleaning up after the event
demanded more personnel than had the event itself.

Urbina drove, confidently whipping the big car
around corners and through streets that were obviously familiar to him. The sight of big jets flying low
and slow served to orient Bolan—they were north of
Miami International Airport and a little west of it.

Soon they were out of Miami and into the flat,
swampy country inland—on the edge of the Everglades. In an area of small factories and warehouses
Bolan spotted what looked like a municipal incinera-
tor. Buildings were low and made of concrete block.
Water stood in ditches along the edges of the roads,
and the occupied land was interspersed with areas of
littered marsh.

"The boonies," Urbina commented.

The buildings became fewer, and Bolan became
aware that they had driven into open country.

Urbina pulled the car off the highway and onto a
rutted road paved only with gravel. The young man
made several more turns until Bolan was aware he'd
have a difficult time finding his way out of the area if
he had to. Then abruptly Urbina stopped the vehicle.
They'd come to a gate in a thicket of thin trees.

The headlights, which Urbina left on, illuminated a
tangle of slender trunks laden with lush parasitic vines.
The undergrowth all but surrounded them. In daylight, Bolan judged, they couldn't have seen more than
ten or fifteen yards in any direction except forward on

the narrow road beyond the gate and back along the road the way they'd come.

It wasn't the kind of situation into which the warrior would have inserted himself, if he'd had the choice. They were clearly visible to anyone watching from back in the bush—visible, that is, to people *they* couldn't possibly see. They were exposed.

He had to assume Iturbe and his two men knew what they were doing. If they didn't, they were fools. Bolan knew that Iturbe was no fool—even so, he couldn't relax.

And suddenly there she was—definitely a she— standing on the road beyond the gate, signaling with her hand for Urbina to put out the headlights, which were blinding her.

He switched off the lights, but in the moment while she stood in the light Bolan had seen a beautiful dark-haired young woman, wearing fatigue pants and a white T-shirt.

She walked forward. It was difficult for Bolan to see her, since his eyes were adjusted to the glare of the headlights, but he saw that she used a key to unlock the chain that held the gate shut. He could see, too, that she was guarded by a formidable German shepherd—a good dog, trained not to bark at the approach of strangers.

Urbina drove through the gate, and the young woman locked it behind them. Iturbe slid over to make room for her in the front seat, and Urbina drove slowly on, without headlights, the big dog trotting beside the car.

Bolan sensed they were being watched from the woods on both sides of the road, though he couldn't hear or see anyone. The quiet air smelled of swamp—of rotting vegetation and the rotting carcasses of fish and animals. Twice he heard big splashes, and he smelled the sharp smell of cigarette smoke—which confirmed that someone was out there, watching.

Men on watch often made a potentially fatal mistake—sentries who smoked didn't realize how far the odor of cigarette smoke could travel, or how distinct it was and how easily recognized. Many a sentry had betrayed himself with his cigarette, thinking that all he had to do was keep the fire hidden. An alert attacker would smell the smoke and then, by checking the wind, figure out where it came from.

So they were being watched. He wasn't surprised. These people weren't here without purpose. Bolan had an idea of what he was going to be shown, what they'd brought him out here to see. And, of course, it would be closely guarded.

The narrow road ended in a clearing, a few hundred square feet of flat, grassy land. Urbina drove across the meadow and brought the Cadillac to a stop under a pair of trees. Everyone got out of the car and headed toward a low building that was located beyond the clearing under some thick, vine-covered trees.

The building was dimly lighted by a single kerosene lantern that sat burning on a table. Bolan could see that from outside, because the building was mostly screen. It had a rusty corrugated steel roof, and was a ramshackle sort of structure that looked more suitable for a big chicken pen than anything else. One room claimed most of the area, though a wooden interior wall suggested there were a couple of small rooms on the side away from the clearing.

Whatever its purpose, the building was out of sight on the ground to anyone fifty yards away from it. From the air it would have been really invisible—even at night, because the weak yellow light from the lantern didn't spill out on the ground or up into the trees.

This was a hideout.

Bolan gained a little more respect for the building as he was led inside. It was more solid than it looked. Besides the table with the lantern, the screened room was furnished with wooden chairs, without upholstery to get wet and rot, or to be occupied by whatever managed to get in through the tight mesh.

There was an ice chest. The young woman opened it and passed everyone a beer.

"Ramona," Iturbe said, "this is the man we call comandante. It's just as well we leave his identification at that."

The woman extended her hand. "Comandante," she said, "my name is Ramona Ramirez."

Bolan shook her hand and felt a firm grip. His first impression of her suggested a plumpish girl, because she was big-boned and stocky. But as he saw her better in the light, he realized she was solid, carrying enough flesh to cover her sturdy frame and none extra. Her eyes were deep and dark, and her black hair hung below her shoulders. Perspiration gleamed on her olive skin.

"You don't need to meet the others now," Iturbe said to Bolan. "They're out there in the night."

"So what am I looking at?" Bolan asked.

"The opposition. We know what we fight. Now you're to see who's going to fight. And with what."

"I see four people," Bolan said.

"There are more."

"Who are going to do what?"

"Fight back," Ramona told him.

"Fight back..." he repeated.

"I mean to kill as many as I can of the snakes who killed my father," Ramona added.

Bolan understood. These people had special reasons.

"What are you organizing, Jorge?" he asked.

"A death squad, comandante," Iturbe replied.

"A *dead* squad, unless you know very well what you're doing."

"We know what we do," Urbina protested.

"One of those guys tonight was firing something heavy and fully automatic," Bolan said. "I took it for an H&K MP-5, and in the hands of a guy who knew how to use it. Heavy stuff. Hard guys." He glanced at the three young people. "Excuse me, but you're kids."

"I'm as old as most of the infantrymen who fought in Vietnam," Urbina said soberly.

With that statement he hit Bolan where he lived. It was true.

"Explanation," Iturbe said.

Bolan nodded. "I'd like to hear one."

Jorge Iturbe smiled sadly. "How does the old curse go? 'May you live in troubled times.' Yes. Live in troubled times. Comandante, we cubanos have always lived in troubled times. Driven from our native land, we made homes in this new one. Then they came after us. Came after us... The worst of them. We were ready to fight back a different way, years ago when you and I first met. We were going to go ashore and drive the snakes off our island. Now we know we'll never go back. Particularly these young ones. They were born here, and they'll never go back. But they've got something they must fight for, just as I did, just as my father did. And they're ready to fight."

"I'll fight the men who murdered my father," Ramona promised.

Bolan nodded. "Okay. You and the ones out in the swamp watching us."

The young woman grinned. She stood and walked to the screen, throwing out her arms in a dramatic signal. Half a dozen young men in camouflage fatigues, carrying heavy weapons, came in from the brush. They stopped at the edge of the clearing, alert.

No question. This was an armed camp. Partly it was kids playing soldier, but not all of them. As Bolan judged Ramona, she was capable of killing as was Tomás. And maybe Homero.

"Jorge," Bolan said, "why did you call me?"

"They need a commander."

"Why not you?" Bolan asked. "Or some other cubano?"

"I have a name," Iturbe replied. "It includes defeat. I'm not sure how much confidence they'd place in me. Besides, I'm more useful where I am. I hear things. I can help. But to be guided by the legendary comandante... Ah, that's something else!"

"'Guided'? Just what do you have in mind, Jorge?"

"These young people are filled with enthusiasm and with purpose. But people who are filled with purpose are often defeated, often badly hurt, because they don't have experience and discipline. What I ask of you, comandante, for old times' sake, is to give these young people the benefit of your wisdom and experience."

Bolan stared into the faces of the solemn young people who sat in the light of the kerosene lantern. They were somber, and they were committed. And if he didn't help them, their commitment might get them killed.

They had a vicious enemy. He'd seen an example of their handiwork at the corner of Coral South and Thirty-first.

If he didn't help them, they'd likely go on without him. And lose. And get killed.

"How many of there are you?" Bolan asked.

"Forty," Urbina replied. "Maybe fifty. A dozen who are committed one hundred percent."

"I like the dozen better," Bolan said. "We might have to ask the others to stand aside."

"Let us show you what we have," Alvarado suggested.

His companions nodded. They moved toward the door, and Bolan put down his beer bottle to accompany them outside.

Alvarado led the way along a narrow trail, away from the clearing and deeper into the swamp. He followed a path that might have been visible in daylight but was invisible now, guided only by the pale glow of a rising moon. The others walked behind him in single file.

He led them to another low building, which lay a little above the waters of the swamp. This one wasn't screened in, but was constructed of corrugated steel. Alvarado opened a giant padlock and slowly swung back the wide door.

Something inside slid away. Snakes loved the insides of buildings such as this, where they could lie in the undisturbed heat. Everyone who knew this kind of country knew better than to walk boldly through a door into a warehouse or long-neglected outbuilding.

When he was inside, the young man switched on a flashlight and searched the darkened corners. Then the others stepped cautiously inside, Iturbe closing the door behind them.

Alvarado bent over a spirit lantern, pumped it up and lit it. The inside of the building filled with brilliant white light.

The place was a warehouse. No. Correctly stated, it was an arsenal. Bolan recognized some of the wooden crates.

Alvarado smiled with evident self-satisfaction as he gestured to Bolan to look at what was stored here.

Okay, what did they have? In the first place, a large supply of 9 mm ammunition—case after case of it. Bolan opened three crates and saw Uzis packed in Cosmoline—submachine guns, mostly, but one crate contained mini-Uzis.

He knew that some other crates contained grenades and plastique.

"What do you plan to do with all this?" he asked Ramona.

"Fight," she replied simply.

"You see the point?" Iturbe asked.

Bolan glanced around the little warehouse. "Not enough. You can't win with just this."

"We know," Ramona agreed.

"This . . . Some of this was accumulated when several of us thought we'd go back to Cuba," Alvarado commented. "Much has had to be discarded. Obsolete. Rusty . . ."

Bolan glanced around the little arsenal one final time, then strode toward the door. "City war," he said. "What are your colleagues going to say, Jorge, when your kids start shooting off these popguns in the streets of Miami?"

"We don't want to fight a war," the detective replied. "That's why we asked you to come, comandante. With your leadership, my 'kids'—as you call them—can carry out a surgical operation that will achieve our purposes without so alarming the city that the police must oppose us."

"You set a tough target, Jorge."

"We fight a difficult fight."

THEY SAT ONCE AGAIN in the screened-in little house, bathed by the yellow light of the lantern.

"All of us," Alvarado said, "are victims." It seemed that Homero Alvarado, not perhaps the best warrior, was the group's spokesman. Also, apparently, he was their armorer—the one who knew more about weapons than any of the rest.

The young man went on. "You have two choices, as we see it. You can try to live with what you are living with. Or you can try to do something about it."

"How are you a victim, Homero?" Bolan asked.

The cubano glanced at the others, then answered, "My brother."

Iturbe took up the story. "His brother was a brave young man. They came to his parents' insurance agency and demanded protection money. His brother broke the nose and jaw of the messenger. A week later they found Homero's brother in a drainage ditch, emasculated before he was shot."

"My family pays the protection now," Alvarado added bitterly. "Even I pretend it's the proper respect to pay to Fraternidad."

"Fraternidad," Ramona went on. "That's what they call themselves. The Brotherhood. The Brotherhood of Cuban Freedom Fighters."

"Cosa Nostra," Alvarado muttered.

"Who are they really?" Bolan probed.

"You can start anywhere," Iturbe said. He glanced at the others. "Why not with Virgilio Gurza? El Padrino. Why not with him?"

"The Godfather?" Bolan said. "That's what he calls himself?"

"*We* call him that," Ramona replied. "We hear it's death for anyone else to call Gurza by the name El Padrino."

"He resents it," Iturbe added. "He thinks it makes him vulnerable. If certain people think his title is godfather—"

"That would be reason enough to kill him," Bolan finished.

"Exactly."

"So if somebody kills him," Bolan guessed, "Fraternidad grows another head, right?"

"It has other heads," Ramona told him. "It wouldn't have to grow one."

"Then where's its vulnerability?" Bolan asked. "What's the key? Where's the weak spot?"

"I'm not sure there is one," Iturbe admitted. "If we thought killing Gurza would kill Fraternidad, we'd go after him. No. We realize we have a big fight on our hands."

3

Tomás Urbina drove Bolan and Iturbe back into the city. They reached police headquarters a little after two in the morning, and the detective checked out another unmarked car.

Iturbe headed north, but before he turned onto the turnpike he stopped at Bolan's hotel, where the warrior picked up the equipment his friend had suggested he'd need for the soft probe to come. Then they entered the turnpike and sped north.

"He lives in Pompano Beach," Iturbe stated. He was briefing Bolan on Virgilio Gurza. "That puts him just a little apart from the action, which is how he wants it. He might be had by a pro, a guy who knows what he's doing and has everything going for him, but he's safe from the occasional outraged cubano who decides to avenge a parent or child."

"Who is the guy, originally?"

"Originally? Originally he was a smart-ass kid on the streets of Havana, a two-bit hoodlum. Then, well, you know who was working Cuba in those days. Meyer Lansky, for one. And others. The Mafia was skimming some important money off operations in Havana. Gurza went to work for those guys. He was

a stone killer, and after a while he got himself made a
wise guy. I mean a full-scale made guy."

"Which isn't bad going for a guy who's not Sicil-
ian," Bolan observed.

"Anyway, the whole crowd got run out of Cuba in
1959. Gurza came out in style, in a helicopter. He
commandeered it with a gun and left a couple of 'men
of respect' on a hotel roof. They swore to have his ass,
but neither of them lived to do it. The story is that
Gurza carried out a bundle of money. American
money. It occupied the seat that one of those senior
guys would have had."

Iturbe stopped while he pulled out and passed a
truck.

"When he got to Florida, he stayed out of circula-
tion for a long time. Lived on the money he'd brought,
learned English, made himself look respectable, got
citizenship. But he kept up his contacts. About twenty
years ago he started to organize what in New York
you'd call a family. And from then on it's the usual
deal."

"How old is he?"

"Sixty, sixty-one. He made his bones in Havana,
but he's made them here, too. He knocked off his opposition."

"So he really is the godfather of southern Florida?"

"Not quite," Iturbe said. "He hasn't got it all under his thumb. Not yet, anyway. A lot of young guys
won't let themselves be organized the way Gurza wants
them organized. They work independently. Plus—
Well, lately you've got the cocaine barons. Gurza

doesn't control them. I figure he's afraid of them. The Colombians, you know. A whole new level of viciousness."

"So you rid yourself of Virgilio Gurza only to get stuck with something worse," Bolan said.

"Not exactly. The coke dealers hurt the people who use their stuff. Gurza hurts the entire cubano community. I mean, he hurts innocent people—people who are just trying to live their lives and get on with things, raise their kids, own homes, have a decent life."

"The old story again," Bolan growled.

"The way I look at it, if you want to place an illegal bet, hire a prostitute, borrow from a loan shark, or buy a line of coke, you take your chances on the guys you have to deal with. You go see them. They don't come see you. But when they get into extortion, selling 'protection,' monopolizing business services, corrupting unions and stuff like that, then *they* come after *you*. And this crowd is blowing people away, just to show how powerful they are. They attacked that squad car tonight, just to show they dare, just to show the town that even the cops aren't safe."

Bolan nodded. "Okay, let's have a look at El Padrino's fort."

FORT LAUDERDALE liked calling itself "the Venice of America." Many hundreds of homes faced the water, most of them on canals. Most of the canals had been excavated and the water allowed to flow in from the bays and streams that dominated the little city. Luxurious homes, surrounded by palm trees and lush tropical vegetation, sat above low sea walls, usually with a boat moored there or hanging on davits. This kind of development continued north into the smaller city of Pompano Beach.

When Jorge left the turnpike at the Pompano Beach interchange and drove east, it was three in the morning.

"I want you to show me the place, then go somewhere and wait for me," Bolan said. "Whatever I'm going to do, I've got to do it alone. I don't want you to be involved in any way."

"Something unofficial?"

"Right. Something unofficial."

The area to which Iturbe took Bolan wasn't the tidily landscaped kind of place most of the canal land in Fort Lauderdale was. This was an area where much of the water was in natural streams and inlets, with not as many straight and walled canals. There were acres of wide open water.

The moon had risen high now, and the Executioner was able to see the house Iturbe pointed out, lying on a low, wooded island of maybe two acres, a hundred yards from the nearest point of land.

Bolan had moved into the back seat, stripped and pulled on a wet suit. "What about security?" he asked. "Electronic sensors?"

The detective shook his head. "I've never been on the island. Nobody from the Pompano police has ever been out there, either. He's got dogs, as I told you. And legbreakers, you can be sure. After that, I don't know."

"Guess we'll find out," Bolan said as he smeared his face with black combat cosmetics.

He strapped on his harness. The Beretta 93-R hung in a watertight holster, and other packets held his knife, a flashlight and other articles of war. A coil of strong nylon rope hung around his left shoulder.

"Go get some coffee," he said to his friend. "This might take a while."

Iturbe had parked at a small public dock, where boats went to and from the several other islands in the inlet. He backed the car away as Bolan lowered himself over the end of the dock and dropped into the water.

It wasn't cold, and the wet suit wasn't really necessary, except that it was black and provided camouflage. He turned toward the island and began to swim, using slow, easy strokes.

About three-quarters of the way across he switched to a breaststroke. It was slower and took more energy, but with it he swam even more quietly, and with his head up. He surveyed the island more closely.

A wooden dock stuck out into the water. Moored on one side was an expensive-looking cabin cruiser, not quite a yacht, but a fast, capable boat. Moored to the other side was what looked like a racing inboard, also a smaller outboard boat.

Lights burned on poles all around the little island. They shone on the ground between the water and the house but also out on the water.

A boat couldn't approach unnoticed. The question was: could a man? He hadn't brought scuba gear, but maybe he should have.

The house was handsome, a one-story white stucco structure with a red tile roof. It had broad picture windows overlooking the water and a big screened-in patio. Lights shone behind about half the windows.

A large dish antenna stood on the roof. Most likely for TV, but perhaps for a sophisticated communications system.

Coming ashore anywhere meant coming ashore in the light. Bolan judged that probably the best approach was to the dock, where he could use the hulls of the boats to block surveillance.

He stopped, treading water, and watched.

A gunman strolled across the lawn and out onto the dock, cradling an assault rifle under his arm. If a man wanted to blow him away, he had set himself up as a conspicuous target. The gunner was followed by a dog, a Doberman, black, lithe, muscular—and dangerous.

The man stopped and stared out across the moonlit water. His eyes passed quickly over the blackened face of the Executioner without spotting him. He turned and walked back toward the house. Bolan saw him slap impatiently at a mosquito, which told the warrior where the guy would probably go: inside the screened-in patio. Bolan lost sight of him, but a moment later a cigarette lighter flamed inside the patio.

The man was inside, but not the dog. The Doberman quietly prowled the outside of the house, a more careful guard than the gunman.

Bolan swam closer. The cabin cruiser was dark, and if anyone was aboard, they were likely asleep.

He swam under the square stern of the boat and reached for and seized the rudder. It was a perfect place to rest, watch and listen.

The tide was out, and the floor of the dock was almost five feet above the surface of the water. Vinyl-covered chain link was nailed to the pilings. Someone didn't want anybody going under there. The mercury-vapor lights on the dock glared as bright as daylight.

He stared at the water's edge. If they had sensors, maybe they were there, a periphery defense.

Yeah. He spotted it. Boxes set on posts at intervals. Beam projectors. They'd project a motion-detecting beam along the edge of the water, probably all around the island. Most likely they'd trained the dog not to go near the water because he, too, would break the beam and set off the alarm. It was a good system.

Bolan floated back out into the water for a few yards to get a better view of the cabin cruiser. He satisfied himself that no one was sitting on the stern deck, waiting for someone to try to climb aboard.

The fact was, the cruiser was outside the defense system for the island.

He swam back to the rudder. In a moment he was up, foot on the rudder, balancing himself and facing the stern deck where, if he'd been wrong, a guy could blast him back into the water. But he was right. In another moment he was aboard, crouched on the deck, alert and wary.

He tried the door to the cabin. It wasn't locked, so he stepped inside. The saloon was outfitted with comfortable chairs, a big television set and a table, which was cluttered with bottles, glasses and the remains of a pizza. The galley was to the left, the head to the right. The bridge was straight on. Sleeping quarters were in the bow: two narrow cabins with bunks. He checked them and found no one.

Okay. He saw the picture. El Padrino traveled to and from the island on this boat. If he was smart—and he almost certainly was smart—he'd vary the routine and sometimes travel some distance along the Inland Waterway before he went ashore. And sometimes he'd travel on one of the smaller boats.

But, like every smart guy, he had trouble with his help. Lying in the open, on the window shelf behind the couch, was a mini-Uzi.

Which corked it. This wasn't some innocent businessman's yacht. If Bolan had had any doubt—which he hadn't really—that settled it. He picked up the little machine pistol. The pizza box had come in a brown paper bag. The warrior tore off a strip of brown paper and used a pencil from the table to jam it down into the short barrel of the Uzi. He shoved hard on the paper until it was a hard mass back near the breech.

Either somebody was careful with weapons—or he wasn't.

Bolan went forward to the bridge. Behind the wheel and other controls he peered out through the glass, looking for a way to get ashore on the island.

He couldn't see any beam sensors at the edges of the dock, but he saw something else. A pole-mounted television camera was focused on the dock. He guessed there would be motion sensors on at least one of the monitor screens inside the house. If anything moved on the dock, it would trigger an alarm.

He'd find a way—there had to be a way. But first a little housekeeping...

The warrior slipped over the rear panel of the cruiser and into the water. He had an idea that had come to him while hanging on to the rudder a few minutes ago. Opening one of the packets on his harness, he removed a small adjustable wrench. Two minutes later the rudder sank to the bottom.

He worked his way around to the other side of the dock. In another two minutes he'd removed the rudder from the fast inboard. He pinched the pin on the outboard, shoved it through and pulled off the propeller. When it sank to the bottom, all three boats were disabled. They wouldn't be able to go after him when he swam away from the island.

Now. How to go ashore?

The warrior swam until he could put his feet down and touch bottom twenty feet to the left of the dock. The decision on how to proceed was taken out of his hands. The Doberman was heading toward him.

The dog walked cautiously, looking around the area, listening keenly, sniffing the air. He was a beautiful, superbly intelligent dog. Bolan could have taken him out with a silent round from the Beretta, but he refused to kill an animal that was only doing what it was trained to do.

He'd come prepared for the encounter. Out of a watertight pouch on his harness he removed an electronic device that generated a powerful but narrow beam of high-pitched sound. Humans couldn't hear it, but dogs could, and it hurt their ears. This was the military version of a gadget invented for joggers—far more powerful and yet not so powerful that the dog would be injured.

The big Doberman began to snarl quietly, and he bared his fangs. He was dangerous, capable of killing. He'd spotted the man in the water and trotted toward him.

Bolan pointed the noise generator at the dog and pressed the button, only for half a second. The warrior heard nothing, but the dog obviously did. He stiffened and shook his head, but didn't retreat. He had located Bolan now, for sure, and he moved closer, emitting a low, threatening growl.

Bolan let him have a longer burst of the painful sound. The Doberman yelped, lowered his head and rubbed his ears on the ground. He rolled over two or three times, then dashed forward and plunged into the water—maybe to attack the source of the painful shriek or maybe out of some sense that the water would ease the hurt in his ears. Anyway, he was in the water only a few yards from Bolan, and the warrior felt he had no choice but to zap him again.

The dog howled in anguish and scrambled onshore. He'd broken the beam, and three gunmen ran from the house.

"Baron! Baron! You damn fool!"

The dog trotted toward the three men, and it was immediately obvious that only one of them was his trainer and that the dog meant to menace the other two. He snarled. But he still shook his head. His ears still hurt.

Bolan swam to the left, fifty yards along the shore of the island. When he put his feet down again, the trainer was rubbing the dog's head, as if he'd at last figured out that the Doberman was somehow in pain. The other men stood apart, their muzzles leveled on the dog—obviously unsure whether or not he was about to attack. Bolan wasn't certain how far the sound from the gadget carried, but he was about to find out.

The three men turned away from the Doberman and walked slowly back toward the house. Bolan aimed and let loose a burst of what had to be a maddening shriek. The Doberman howled and again ran for the water. He broke the beam, and the alarm went off again.

The warrior walked through the beam fifty yards away, setting off another alarm indistinguishable from the one the dog made. What was more, the three men running toward the dog failed to notice that a man in black had walked out of the water, across the grass strip between the water and the shrubbery around the house and was now at large on the island.

THE ALARM WAS SILENT. It didn't set off a howling horn or flashing lights. All it did was discreetly alert the gunmen in the house that something had tripped the alarm. A bird did it from time to time, perhaps small animals coming ashore.

Now the question was, how good were they? If the gunners were very good, at least one man remained quietly inside. It would be foolhardy for every man to go running out to the water's edge every time the alarm went off. That would leave the house undefended.

Likely, then, somebody stayed behind, watching from inside.

Another thing to consider was the question of whether there was another line of alarm sensors closer to the house. Bolan judged not. The dog moved freely on the grounds.

The house and grounds occupied about half the land of the island. The screened-in patio was on the south end of the house; the dock was on the east side of the island. Bolan crouched in the shadow of a big flowering bush not far from the southeast corner of the patio.

The gunmen led the Doberman back to the house and took him inside the patio. The dog continued to snarl and shake his head. He knew where Bolan was, but he was also smart enough to identify this intruder with the pain in his ears, and he complained only generally, not barking in the direction where the warrior crouched and watched.

"What's the matter with Baron?" one of the gunmen grunted.

The trainer answered, "I don't know. Something's spooking him. Maybe there's an alligator out there."

"Should we wake somebody up?"

"You kidding? If you want to wake up the old man to tell him there's an alligator in the water, go ahead."

Bolan could see them in there. He was under the lights that flooded the lawn, but they sat without lights and, of course, had a clear view of the whole lighted area.

"Sorry about this, Baron," the warrior whispered as he pressed the button and gave the Doberman another shot of pain. "I don't know what I'd have done without you."

Inside the screened-in patio the dog began to howl and writhe. As the men stared at him—all but the trainer a little scared—Bolan trotted unnoticed across the south side of the house and around the corner to the west. He took cover under a flowering shrub for a moment, then moved on while the confusion inside continued. In a moment he was beyond the limit of the patio and was on the back side of the house proper.

The outside unit of the air-conditioning system was running, the fan blowing hot air toward the water. The noise was enough to cover a man's movements, if they needed covering.

Bolan moved past the air conditioner and reached the back door.

Here was another place where they might have an alarm. He had his retreat prepared—that is, he had disabled their boats—so he decided to try the door. If he set off an alarm, he could be across the back lawn and into the water in seconds, and once he was in the water they couldn't follow him except by swimming, which he doubted any of them would try.

He turned the knob.

Nothing.

He opened the door and walked into the kitchen.

In a minute or so he understood the layout of the house. The kitchen, dining room and living room were all on the south end of the house. Wide glass doors separated the big living room from the patio. The

bedrooms were all on the north end. In one of them—
the biggest, the most luxurious—El Padrino slept.

The door between the kitchen and dining room wa
open. To his right he could see through the dinin,
room and living room, all the way to the patio, wher
the trainer now knelt beside the Doberman and wa
trying to comfort him. To Bolan's left a hall ran to :
door on the north end of the house. The bedroom
would lie on both sides of that hall.

Which bedroom would be Gurza's? Bolan was will
ing to guess. It would be at the front of the house
overlooking the dock—and farthest from the noisy ai
conditioner that ran in the backyard. The first tw
doors off the hall and on the front side weren't very fa
apart. He guessed those opened into small bedrooms
probably used by the gunmen. Slipping down the hall
he came to paneled double doors with heavy bras
hardware. That would be it.

He turned one of the big brass handles and pushe
the door. A night light in the adjoining bathroor
filled the big bedroom with dim yellow light. Virgili
Gurza, a fat, bald man, lay sprawled in sleep, sprea
halfway over a king-size bed. He was naked, and s
was the girl who slept beside him. Bolan frowned
He'd be surprised if she was more than seventeen year
old.

He stepped across the room and stood for a mc
ment, staring at Gurza. If what Iturbe and the other
said of him was true, he deserved a bullet between th
eyes here and now. But Mack Bolan wasn't a kille
who blew men away without ever having seen the evi
dence that made them deserve it. This guy was sur

rounded by tight security, and he was sleeping with an underage female... but death wasn't the penalty for that.

For now Bolan would just shake Gurza, shake him hard and see what happened.

It was what he'd had in mind from the time he'd decided to come out to this island, and he was carrying what he needed. It hung on a chain around his neck—a sharpshooter medal, a token of a visit from the Executioner.

The warrior pulled it out of the wet suit and off his neck. He bent over Gurza, lay the medal on his chest and draped the chain over and behind his head. The man didn't stir. Bolan pressed down on the pillow and gave the chain a little tug. Again Gurza didn't waken, and now the chain was around his neck.

But the girl woke. She suddenly opened her eyes and looked up in terror at the big man with the blackened face. The warrior put his left hand firmly but gently on her mouth, placed his right index finger to his lips, smiled at her and shook his head. The girl gagged as if she was about to vomit, but she didn't scream.

Bolan backed across the room and out the bedroom door. He could hear the girl begin to cry, and heard Gurza grumble.

The warrior trotted along the hall and out the north door, pursued by a bellow of rage from Gurza. He dashed across the lawn in front of the house and onto the dock. At the end of the dock he dived into the water.

When he surfaced and looked back, he could see the gunmen sprinting across the lawn. He swam hard to put distance between him and them, even if his splashing would show them where he was.

The first man who reached the end of the dock fired a burst of slugs. Bolan had expected that and dived to the bottom. The burst hit far beyond where he'd been. A man in the water, in the dark, wasn't an easy target, and this gunman was overanxious.

Two others leaped aboard the cruiser. One ran to the bridge and started the engine while the other cast off the line. The man on the bridge spun the wheel and shoved in the throttles. Without a rudder the boat surged forward and rammed hard against a pile of rocks.

The man who had cast off the lines grabbed the mini-Uzi in the cabin, ran out to the stern and leveled the muzzle toward the man in the water fifty yards out. This was the Uzi with the paper jammed down the barrel. When the gunman pulled the trigger, the machine pistol blew up.

Others had discovered by now that the remaining two boats were disabled. They climbed onto the dock and tried to pick off the swimmer with bursts from their assault rifles, but it was a rare marksman who could hit a small target at any great distance.

Bolan made himself a small target. Diving and swimming underwater, surfacing and stroking a while, then ducking under again, he swam out of their range and out of sight.

4

Virgilio Gurza had pulled on a pair of white shorts. He sat on a stool in the kitchen, a heavy-bellied figure resembling a carving of an ancient Chinese laughing god. He'd lighted a cigar and now sat scowling at the man with the injured hands.

"Smart," he muttered. "The pistol blows up. The boat hits the rocks. The outboard's on the bottom. Even the stupid dog doesn't do what he's supposed to do. And the son of a bitch got in my bedroom! Right in my goddamn *bedroom* and hung a medal around my neck!"

Gurza glanced at the blonde. She had on panties and a bra and sat at the kitchen table drinking gin on the rocks. "Mary Lou, you'll get a hangover," he grumbled.

"I've *got* a hangover already, which is why I need a drink."

"Lucky girl," said the man who held his arms and hands in front of him on the table in a pile of bloody towels. The girl held the glass of gin to his lips, and the man drank.

"They got the rudder back on," Gurza said. "The doc'll be here soon. So tell me, why the hell did you shoot out over the water like there was a war? If I've got to answer for that, some guy's ass is in a sling."

The man whose hands had been severely hurt by the explosion of the mini-Uzi nodded at Mary Lou and tossed his head, indicating he wanted more gin. "What's that medal?" he asked.

"I wish I could think it's not what I think it is," Gurza replied, "but I've heard of this. Other guys have got these, and they didn't live to wish they had tighter security."

"In other words..." the dog trainer prompted.

Gurza sighed and pondered for a moment. "Well, maybe you're not so dumb. Maybe... If this is what I think it is, we've got shit like we never thought of before. There's a guy who goes around wasting guys who are trying to set things up their way. For no reason. He's some kind of goddamn nut."

"He could of killed you easy," said the man with the injured hands. "So why didn't he?"

Gurza picked up the medal. "A warning. This is some kind of warning," he said quietly.

"So what do we do?"

"We've got two choices," Gurza replied. "We get out of business and blow, or we get this son of a bitch!"

"Get the son of a bitch," the dog trainer said. "How tough could it be?"

"He got past you tonight," Gurza snarled. "You and your smart-ass dog. You tell me how tough he is. You tell me how smart he is. He was in my goddamn bedroom! He could of cut my throat...and Mary Lou wouldn't even have woken up. Drunken broad. How tough could it be, huh? How tough do you figure?"

"I want him," the man with injured hands said.

"Yeah, well, is that the way I read it? You guys want to go after that guy? You got the guts, or are you afraid of him? The other way is to take what we got and blow."

"What do you want to do, boss?"

"We're going to get that guy." He looked around. Nobody disagreed. "So how? How do we find him? How do we get him?"

VIRGILIO GURZA WAITED until midmorning, then called New York. The man he wanted to talk to wasn't available, but later, a little before noon, the man called. Gurza described his problem.

"You got a problem," the man in New York told him. "A real problem. All I can tell you is that there's a million bucks waiting for whoever whacks that guy. Listen, the X has been on him for a long time. Put the word out. One mill, cool, to the guy who gives that son of a bitch the big headache."

"I suppose a lot of guys have tried."

The man in New York laughed. "Lots of guys."

"What's he into?" Gurza asked. "Broads? Booze? Action? Nose candy?"

"All of them, I suppose," the man in New York replied. "Except maybe the nose candy. He's some kind of guy, the word is. But you won't take him out easy. Some good men have tried."

"I hear you," Gurza said unhappily, and hung up.

MACK BOLAN SLEPT four hours, then went to the coffee shop for some breakfast. Jorge Iturbe came in while he was eating.

"Don't want to stick to you like glue, comandante," he began, "but I don't suppose you know your way around the cubano community."

"I want to see a protection man," Bolan said.

"I'm going to see to it you get to see a protection seller, but not with me. I'm a cop, and I'm known. I'm going to send one of my kids to show you around. How about you wait in your room?"

"Right."

He could use some more sleep, and he was stretched out on the bed, dozing lightly, when he heard a firm rap on the door. He opened it and saw that Iturbe had sent Ramona. Why?

She spoke the answer, as if she'd expected the question. "The boys have jobs and I don't work. Not now, anyway. Jorge figures I'm less conspicuous."

If Iturbe figured that, he was all wrong. The woman was wearing a pair of tight, well-worn and well-faded blue jeans slung low across her hips so that her navel was bare. Above, she was wearing the halter half of a yellow bikini in which her breasts hung loosely, neither confined nor completely covered. She was wearing her hair tied in a ponytail, and a pair of aviator sunglasses was perched on top of her head.

She looked very young, and very much like a girl looking for fun.

"Dress something like me," she said, "and carry your gun in a beach bag."

She opened her own stylish beach bag and let him see, nestled between two towels, a Beretta 92-F. She had fifteen rounds of 9 mm ammo in a thoroughly reliable and accurate pistol.

"I've got no place to hide it," she said, turning around, showing how tightly her jeans clung to her rear.

"I noticed that."

"If you've got no beach bag, I've got an extra one in the car. Put whatever you want to bring in here, and we can transfer in the car."

"Deal," he said.

He put his own Beretta in beside hers and noticed her looking at it with critical interest. Apparently the lady knew something about weapons.

He dressed in a pair of jeans as faded as hers and a red T-shirt. Then he put on sunglasses like hers and a Red Sox baseball cap.

Her car was a Volkswagen Rabbit convertible, and the top was down. Seated beside Ramona, Bolan shifted his pistol into the second red beach bag and settled it between his legs. He kept the bag unzipped so that he'd have easy access to the Beretta if he needed it.

The motel was on the edge of a cubano neighborhood, so Ramona didn't have far to drive to where the warrior would be able to see some of Gurza's muscle at work. The streets here were clearly cubano. Signs were in Spanish: *Bodega, Florero, Farmacia, Zapatería, Almacén*—grocery, florist, pharmacy, shoe shop, department store.

"Soon," Ramona said, "there'll be no more signs in the old language. As the old ones die off."

"You speak English as well as I do. No accent."

She shrugged. "I was taught in an American school, and in those days you spoke English in the schoolroom or you didn't speak at all. Now we have bilingual education, but—" She shrugged. "We study Spanish now the way the Irish study Gaelic. Something from the past. Makes the old people happy. I'm an American."

Turning a corner, she accelerated. They all but raced through a block. "The bakery on the right."

The sign painted on the glass said Panadería, but there was no bakery there. Not anymore.

"That was my father's bakery. They killed him. They demanded he receive shipments of cocaine in the bags of sugar that came in from Mexico, and they wanted him to order five times the sugar he needed and let them sift it when it arrived to find the condoms filled with cocaine. He wouldn't do it and they killed him. My mother has gone to live in Houston. Nobody dares buy the bakery's ovens, the cases where he displayed his pastry, and nobody dares rent the building. My mother is forced to live on her sister's charity."

"And you mean to kill Gurza," Bolan concluded.

"Jorge tells me you could have killed him last night and didn't," she said bitterly.

"Cut off a head, another grows. Why not let him sweat a little? He doesn't feel comfortable this morning and isn't as confident as he was this time yesterday. We'll get him when the time is right."

RAMONA DROVE through one neighborhood after another.

"You think they're out with signs on their backs?" she asked. "I don't see anybody I can identify. Anyway, I can't identify more than one or two of them."

"Who killed your father?" Bolan asked.

"Are you interested?"

"You're damn right."

Ramona took a deep breath, which she expelled slowly. "Okay. I thought you'd never ask. Jorge gave me strict orders not to tell you. A sideshow, he says. But since you asked . . ."

"I asked."

"Alberto Angeles is the one who talked to my father about bringing in the cocaine in his sugar. Maybe Angeles didn't kill my father, but after my father refused the guy's demand, he was shot to death on the sidewalk in front of his bakery. Angeles is the one who sent around the word that anyone who buys anything that belonged to the Ramirez bakery is his enemy."

"Are you sure about all this, Ramona?"

"I swear," she replied.

"Okay. Show me where to find him, then go home. I'll tell you what happened after it happens."

"Bullshit," she said simply.

"Ramona, I work alone, or I don't work at all. Not on this."

The woman stared at him for a long moment, angry, making a judgment. Then she sighed. "I'll show you." She drove him north, then east.

The neighborhoods were the same—too few trees, too little green. A white tropical sun burning on streets and buildings. In more prosperous parts of the city the landscaping was constantly watered, kept wet and green. Here, no one cared enough to spend the money, so the greenery wilted and scorched, and hot, dry dust swirled in the weak wind.

"Fill me in on Angeles."

"He came to Florida about ten years ago," she said. "Fidel let him go—he let the worst ones go. Or maybe he works for Fidel. We can't be sure. Anyway, he's a member of Fraternidad. If Gurza is a godfather, Angeles is a capo. He uses terrorist tactics. It makes you wonder where he learned his lessons. Maybe with Che Guevara."

"Terrorist. Besides murdering your father—"

"An ordinary criminal would have given my father a second chance." Ramona shrugged. "My father would have refused the second time, too. But they didn't ask a second time. They never do. They would have killed me if they could, and they tried. We didn't dare even have a funeral. The undertaker was afraid to take the body. The priest did the last rites at the morgue. Jorge arranged that. Even the Mafia allow people a goddamn funeral!"

Bolan nodded sympathetically and tried to change the subject. "What does he look like?"

"Like a greaseball. Lots of black hair with enough oil on it to lubricate an eight-cylinder engine. Dark eyes in dark circles, like he wears eye shadow. A sneer. He's got a good body—he works out with weights. He wears Latino shirts—you know, all fluffy and embroidered, tail out. If you see him, you'll know him."

"Okay. Where am I going to find him?"

"I'll take you there. He'll be sitting on his little throne, presiding over his court."

ALBERTO ANGELES did, in fact, preside over a sort of court, a squalid congregation of hard-looking men in a run-down cantina.

Bolan wouldn't go inside until Ramona's Volkswagen disappeared in the distance. Then he walked in, carrying the red beach bag with the Beretta nestled in the folds of a towel.

The inhabitants checked him out, but they saw nothing menacing, apparently, in the big man who walked up to the bar and ordered a beer. After a hard look, the men returned their attention to their boss, Alberto Angeles.

The man was very much as Ramona had described him. He wore a fancy embroidered shirt, white-on-white, tail out. He smoked a thin cigar, and looked comfortable and content with himself.

He was attended by three hardguys who hung on his every word. A bottle of red wine sat on their flimsy wooden table. They spoke a Cuban dialect. Bolan could understand a few words, but he couldn't follow the rapid, idiomatic conversation.

Sipping at his beer, the warrior surreptitiously glanced around the cantina. The hardguys treated Angeles with exaggerated respect. It wasn't hard to see that they were afraid of him. They knew him well, but even someone who didn't could see something in his eyes that said "cruel," that said this man could be totally ruthless.

Bolan had run into this kind of man before. The world was full of them.

"*¿Otro cerveza?*" the bartender asked.

"*Sí,*" Bolan replied.

A word had come into the conversation at the table. *Medalla,* medal. Then the name Gurza. They were talking about the medal El Padrino had found around his neck.

The Executioner shoved his half-full beer bottle across the bar and pushed three dollar bills after it. Then he slipped off the bar stool and walked over to Angeles's table.

Bolan hooked a toe around the chair that was vacant, jerked it out and sat down. "Alberto Angeles, I suppose."

The men stiffened.

"*¿Quién está usted?*" Angeles asked with menace in his voice.

"Speak English, jerk!" Bolan demanded, hoping to get a reaction.

The hardguy to Angeles's right was quick. In barely an instant he had his knife out and arcing toward Bolan's throat. A silenced round from the warrior's Beretta 93-R ripped through the wooden tabletop and drilled into the hardguy's chest just as the knife skimmed across Bolan's throat.

The knife man flopped back and slid down to the floor, upsetting his chair. The others didn't know where the muzzle under the table pointed now. No one dared to move.

Bolan nodded at one of the hardguys. He flipped his head to one side, telling the man to move. The man moved, sliding off his chair and walking decisively toward the door. Then the warrior gave the same gesture to the other guy, with the same result.

The Executioner was left facing Angeles. He checked the bartender, who was making a point of keeping his hands on the bar. The other men at the bar tried to pretend they'd seen nothing.

Bolan drew the Beretta from underneath the table, shoved it into the waistband of his jeans, then stood. "I understand you're a big man. The name's Angeles, right?"

Angeles stood and held his hands out to his sides in a gesture of surrender. "What do you want?" Then, without warning, he leaped across the table, hands outstretched toward Bolan's throat.

The warrior kicked the table out from between them and drove a fist into Angeles's nose. He felt the cartilage disintegrate, the nose collapse. Thrown back against the wall, Angeles grabbed for his pant pocket. He managed to draw a tiny automatic before Bolan's hard-driven fist found his jaw. Then, before the cubano could raise the muzzle of the automatic, Bolan's knee crunched into his crotch, crushing his scrotum.

Angeles went weak and dropped the automatic. As he staggered to one side, Bolan's next punch broke his jaw. The man sprawled facedown on the floor, moaning.

The Executioner glanced alertly around the cantina. He picked up the red beach bag. Then from his pocket he withdrew a marksman's medal, which he tossed to Angeles's feet. "Tell him he's out of business," he said to the bartender. "Tell him he's retired."

THE CUT ON HIS THROAT wasn't painful, but it was still bleeding a little when Bolan returned to his motel. He turned the key in the lock and was confronted by Ramona, who was sitting in the armchair facing the door.

"You're hurt."

"Not bad."

The knife had broken the skin, nothing more, and had bled as a cut to the throat does, but he was right in saying it wasn't a serious injury.

Ramona grabbed his arm and pulled him toward the bathroom. She had anticipated he might come back wounded, and she was ready with a first-aid kit. "Sit down," she told him curtly.

He sat on the closed lid of the toilet, and Ramona washed his wound, bathed it with antiseptic and finally bandaged it.

"Did you get Angeles?" she asked.

"We exchanged a few blows," the warrior replied dryly.

"But he's still alive? What are you trying to do, comandante, just make enemies? You let another one live?"

"There's a saying," he told her, "that goes like this—'who the gods would destroy they first make mad.'"

She shook her head. "'Whom God would destroy He first sends mad.' Meaning insane. Making these guys howling furious isn't going to do it."

"Insanely angry. Men who get angry do stupid things."

Ramona sat on the edge of the bathtub. "Hurt?"

He shook his head.

"Good." She reached behind and unfastened her bikini halter, dropping it to the floor. She stood and began to pull down her jeans.

"Ramona, I—"

"Shh." She placed her fingers across his lips. "You need a couple hours' rest. I intend to see that you get it. Later."

5

When Bolan awakened, the room was bathed in sunlight. Because the air-conditioning worked only marginally, they lay uncovered, letting any tiny breath of air blow across them. Ramona lay on her back, sound asleep.

But sudden waking meant trouble. It always did. The warrior rarely slept deeply. Some sounds passed by, others jerked him awake.

Bolan rolled off the bed, grabbing the Desert Eagle as he went. He rose into a crouch, the big .44 Magnum already leveled at the door.

He reached for Ramona, meaning to jerk her off the bed to the floor, but then, as a long-honed sense had told him would happen, the door erupted in an explosion of wood, flying ahead of a burst of heavy slugs.

The gunner had aimed a little high, the stream of steel chopping the wall just above Ramona. The blasted-out hole in the door indicated the man's position as vividly as if Mack Bolan had had X-ray vision. The muzzle was behind the hole, and the gunman was behind the muzzle.

The Executioner fired just once—through the hole already blown in the wooden door. A quick burst drilled into the ceiling, the last reflexive act of a dying man.

Terrified, Ramona had sat up.

"Down!" Bolan yelled.

She was quick, rolling off the bed on the side opposite Bolan just as a second stream of slugs thudded into the mattress. But another gunman had made the same mistake as his companion. Slugs blasted through the plaster of the wall, locating the gunner as precisely as if he'd painted his outline on the wall. Bolan fired a second .44 Magnum slug at the jagged hole, and the gunman screamed.

"They followed you!" Ramona wailed.

"And took a little time to get their troops together," Bolan muttered. "It's not over."

Ramona crawled around the foot of the bed, clutching her Beretta in her right hand.

"Their move, Ramona," he said. "And plan on another move. Get into the bathroom and into the tub. The steel—"

"No, goddamn it. I'm not going to hide while you fight."

She shrieked and pointed. A bomb had been tossed onto the balcony just outside their room—three sticks of dynamite, enough to blow them to shreds. It hit against the sliding glass door, fuse smoking, fire speeding toward the blasting cap.

Bolan spun and fired the Desert Eagle. A bullet hitting the dynamite would have set it off as surely as the blasting cap, but he'd aimed a foot higher. The glass of the door shattered under the impact of the big high-velocity slug, and it fell in a cascade. Bolan jumped to the door and gave the dynamite bomb a kick. It arced out over the parking lot and fell.

The Executioner threw himself on top of Ramona, and the debris propelled in by the blast—brick and plaster and glass—swept over him, cutting and stinging.

In the instant after the storm of debris Ramona was on her feet. She grabbed her clothes but didn't pause to put them on. *"Now!"* she yelled.

Bolan scrambled to his feet, dazed by the force of the blast and the hurricane of debris that had struck him. He rushed into the hall, tracking the muzzle of the Desert Eagle right and left, ready to fire on anyone who challenged them. He saw two corpses, the gunmen who'd blasted the door and wall.

Ramona stepped back into the room and let loose half a dozen slugs through the gap where window and wall had been. She picked up Bolan's clothes and grabbed the beach bag that contained his Beretta and other possessions and ran into the hall.

"Car..." she gasped. She pointed toward the front of the motel. "There are too many of them to fight! They'll figure it all out pretty soon!"

Dressing on the run, they jumped over the body of one of the gunmen and sprinted toward the entrance of the motel. A moment later they burst into the lobby. Terrified staff and guests of the establishment cowered on the floor as the gun-toting man and woman raced past.

The Volkswagen sat in a parking place in front of the building. As Ramona ran for it, Bolan stood spread-eagle on the pavement just beside it, ready to fire on anybody who moved to interfere with their escape.

Ramona started the engine, and Bolan leaped into the front seat. The gunmen knew where they were now. Bullets spanged off the pavement around them as Ramona jammed the accelerator to the floor and the Volkswagen shot out of the lot. In a minute the vehicle was free and speeding away.

Ramona drove to the Everglades camp where Bolan had met her two nights earlier. In the screened-in main room of the building she swabbed his cuts with antiseptic and covered a few of them with bandages. A young man in camouflage fatigues stained with sweat came in to help, but wandered off into the swamp as soon as he saw that everything was under control.

Ramona popped the tops of two cans of beer and handed one to Bolan, then lit the lantern. "Too close," she commented as she sat down in one of the wooden chairs. "They almost got us."

"That's why I work alone."

"You can't work alone. You don't know these people and where to find them."

"I'll find them," he promised. "Right now I've got *them* looking for *me*."

She glanced at her wristwatch, saw that it was time for the seven o'clock news and switched on the battery-powered radio. The attack on the motel was the headline story. The dynamite blast had injured half a dozen people—fortunately none of them seriously. The announcer described how an armed man and woman had run through the lobby and into the parking lot, then sped away in a car.

"The room was rented in the name of Michael Blanski, who gave a Baltimore address. He paid for his room with cash in advance, for three nights. Baltimore police say the address is a phony, and it seems likely Blanski isn't the man's real name. His fingerprints have been taken and will be sent to the FBI."

Ramona frowned. "They'll identify you."

"No, they won't." She didn't challenge the statement.

The announcer went on to describe what he called a shooting in a cantina in a cubano neighborhood.

"Witnesses say the shooting was unprovoked and can only assume it was for revenge over some personal matter. The killer proceeded to beat a witness. Alberto Angeles, a businessman, is hospitalized with broken facial bones and other injuries."

"They don't make the connection."

"The guys who count make it," Bolan said.

JORGE ITURBE ARRIVED about eight, followed by Homero Alvarado and Tomás Urbina.

The detective handed Mack Bolan a roll of bills. "Here's a thousand dollars. When you guys took off from that motel room, you left your money. Not to mention your belongings." He nodded at the suitcase Urbina had carried in. "I think what's in there will fit you. Also, there's a razor, shaving soap...things like that. You left your wet suit and other equipment in my car last night, fortunately, and I see you got away with both your guns."

"First things first," Ramona said.

"Thanks." Bolan frowned at the money. "Who—"

"A couple of honest businessmen." Iturbe waved a hand, dismissing the subject. "I saw that motel room. You're both lucky to be alive."

Bolan nodded toward Ramona. "Tell her to stay away from me."

"You went after your personal revenge, Ramona," Iturbe said sternly. "Now you've got 'em on your ass. The little red Volkswagen Rabbit, it's dead. That's how they found the comandante this afternoon. They sent guys around to motels looking for your car. They've made the connection between you and the guy they're calling Blanski. If you want my advice, you'll stay here and out of the city until the comandante's work is finished and he's gone. And maybe you won't be safe even then."

"I haven't been safe," she said sullenly, "since the day my father refused to accept their shipments of cocaine."

"Only now the danger is ten times greater," he said. "You've just been moved to the top of their list, Ramona—right under the comandante."

"An honor," she muttered.

"Not an honor!" Iturbe yelled, slamming his hand on the table. "What if they followed the red Volkswagen out here? It's not an honor, and it's not smart to get so much attention."

Ramona's jaw trembled, as though she were fighting back sobs.

"You got your revenge," he went on. "You talked El Comandante into getting it for you. You risked his life, and you risked your own. Not to mention ours. From now on, Ramona, you take orders. You carry out what you're directed to carry out. No more projects of your own. Or get out."

She dropped her gaze and remained silent.

"I said I wanted to see a protection seller," Bolan informed him.

The detective nodded. "So she showed you Gurza's number two or number three man for her own motives. Well, what you did last night was far more important. Virgilio Gurza is a badly frightened man."

"Maybe he should have another visit tonight."

"He's not there."

"We should keep the pressure on," Bolan suggested. "Where's a good pressure point?"

"Octavo Marzo," Alvarado said quietly.

"A yacht," Iturbe added. "The Eighth of March, named for Virgilio Gurza's birthday. It was handed to him as a birthday gift four years ago. An expensive present, even for Fraternidad. Some people think it was really a gift from Fidel."

"It goes to Cuba," Ramona said.

"We think it does," Iturbe corrected her. "We can't be sure, one way or the other. It goes south, cruises along the Cuban coastline but well outside Cuban territorial waters. It's doubtful they really go in. More likely they rendezvous."

"What are they doing, smuggling cocaine?"

Iturbe shook his head. "The Coast Guard has stopped it at least a dozen times. They've searched it from the keel to the radar antenna and have never found anything illegal. All the boat seems to be used for is partying. When they're asked why they go so close to Cuba, they say the fishing is good there—and, besides, they have a sentimental wish to stare through binoculars at the old homeland.''

"Tell the comandante about Manuela Lopez," Ramona suggested, bitterness in her voice.

The detective drew a deep breath. "Manuela Lopez was an undercover agent of the Drug Enforcement Agency. She volunteered to get herself aboard *Octavo Marzo* to get a close look at what was going on. We don't know whether she managed to get aboard or not, but she disappeared at the same time that the yacht sailed out of Biscayne Bay and headed south. Three weeks later her body washed ashore on Key Largo.''

"It had been in the water a long time," Ramona added. "She'd drowned. Of course, no one can prove she was thrown overboard from *Octavo Marzo*. But what else could have happened?"

"You can just assume—" Jorge began.

"What about surveillance of this boat?" Bolan interrupted. "Is it watched?"

"It's been shadowed on the surface and from the air several times," Iturbe told him, "but the Coast Guard and the DEA can't give over the resources it would take to tail it every time it goes to sea. There are too many other demands for personnel and equipment. So it's watched sometimes. Random checks.''

"Nobody goes aboard but members of Fraternidad," Alvarado said. "Even the crew. If it happened to sink, no innocent person would drown."

"A pressure point," Bolan concluded.

THE YACHT WAS DOCKED on the Middle River in Fort Lauderdale—far enough from Gurza's island home so as not to be identified too easily with him, not so far away as to be inconvenient. Alvarado and Urbina knew where it was, had seen it often and could identify it.

Bolan and the two young cubanos drove to Lauderdale in an old Ford pickup truck, once painted bright red but now only a chalky pink.

At Bolan's suggestion the two men has shed their combat fatigues and put on blue jeans and T-shirts, as well as country straw hats. They looked like migrant fruit pickers, which was what the warrior intended. No one would have guessed they carried Beretta 92-Fs in the wadded-up blue denim jackets that lay between their feet on the floor of the pickup's cab.

"This is recon, don't forget," Bolan said when the truck turned into the street that led to the dock. "We're not trying to take him out. Soft probe. Okay?"

They drove along a beautiful waterfront street on a canal where luxurious yachts were drawn up in line along the docks. At this hour—after midnight—almost no one was active on the dock, though many of the big boats were lighted and people sat on the rear decks, smoking and drinking. Here and there a couple of men worked on a boat—hosing it down, tuning an engine, making ready to take a fishing party out early in the morning.

"*Octavo Marzo...*" Alvarado said, pointing at a vacant space on the dock. "It's not here!"

Jorge Iturbe could confirm it in a few minutes. While Bolan waited in a telephone booth, the detective called the Coast Guard.

"*Octavo Marzo* left the dock sometime a little after ten," he said. "It's on its way down the Intracoastal. Correction. It's in Biscayne Bay. It passed the Seventy-ninth Street Causeway about half an hour ago. She's going to sea, comandante—beyond any doubt."

"With Gurza aboard?" Bolan asked.

"Who knows? But look, if you want to follow the yacht, have the boys drive you to Homestead as quickly as possible. I'll have a boat ready for you there. Who's driving? Tomás? Tell him Princeton Pier. You can make five times the speed *Octavo Marzo* can make."

"We'll be there in about an hour."

"Yeah. Probably forty-five minutes. Don't plan on going to sea the minute you get there. These deals take a little time."

IT TOOK an hour and a quarter to reach the pier. And then, what was there waiting for them, with Iturbe standing on the dock surveying it skeptically, was a fishing boat—a little old, a little scarred, with a conspicuously sleepy man checking the tanks. The boat was named *Islamorada*.

"Meet Jesús Rodriguez," the detective said to Bolan. "This is Jesús's boat."

Bolan shook hands with Rodriguez, who was an oversize man, with the muscles of a boxer, his white nautical cap shoved down on what looked like a shaved head. He wore a ragged white T-shirt, cut off halfway up to the armpits, which exposed his muscular torso and the navel above the waistband of his jeans.

Rodriguez grinned. "No fishing, hmm? Good. I'm bored with fishing, bored with fishermen, bored most of all with their wives. You want to trail *Octavo Marzo?* Okay, if he doesn't throttle in. If he does that, we can't keep up. But he doesn't know the waters as well as I do. There's more than one way to keep up."

The big man went about checking his boat, and Jorge Iturbe talked earnestly with Bolan.

"It's the best I could get on short notice. But don't worry about him. He's good. Between you and me—something nobody else knows—he's done work for the DEA. He's got guts, comandante, and he's got guns on board. I mean, heavy stuff."

Bolan surveyed the boat and was skeptical. But he liked Rodriguez. The warrior stepped from the dock and boarded the boat.

"Okay," Iturbe said. "Since we talked on the phone, *Octavo Marzo* passed through the Rickenbacker Causeway." He nodded toward the sea. "She's out there right now. One of those lights could be her."

Bolan turned and looked at the dim lights out on the night ocean.

"There's something else, comandante. Join me below."

Bolan followed as Iturbe walked forward from the open rear deck into the cabin, then down into the single lower cabin where the bunks were.

A young woman sat on a bench, running a rod through the barrel of a mini-Uzi. "Comandante," she said.

It was Ramona, but her long dark hair had been cut and was short, stiff, bleached. She wore combat fatigues and heavy boots.

"She brought weapons," Iturbe said.

"In the fatal red Volkswagen," she added, "then shoved it off the end of the dock. Jesús was amazed, but the dear little Rabbit sleeps with the fishes. I brought guns, ammo and grenades. Good stuff."

"Don't tell her to get off on the dock," the detective warned. "We'd have to haul her off, kicking and screaming."

Bolan shrugged. "She's a fighter."

6

The rising sun had turned the eastern sky milky gray when *Islamorada* finally pulled away from the dock and headed out into the broad, choppy waters of the southern reaches of Biscayne Bay.

A radio transmission from the Coast Guard to the Miami police, passed on by Jorge Iturbe just before *Islamorada* cast off, said that *Octavo Marzo* had passed through the strait between Old Rhodes Key and Key Largo and then turned south. This put the yacht more than twenty miles ahead.

Rodriguez showed Bolan the chart. "If we take a chance here, we can catch up, maybe get ahead. If he's on his way to Cuban waters, he's going to go down the southeast side of the Keys. If we go down the northwest side a ways, we'll gain on him because the water's calmer. It's up to you."

"It's up to the man who knows the boat and the waters," Bolan replied.

Rodriguez grinned. "I recommend we take the chance."

He steered south into Card Sound, under the bridge into Barnes Sound, on through the passage into Blackwater Sound and out into Florida Bay. In the brilliant red light of a spectacular sunrise, *Islamorada*

hurned south, making good speed among small sandy
islands and through hordes of fishing boats coming
out as the day dawned.

Iturbe had driven back to Miami, and Alvarado had
driven the truck back to the camp in the Everglades.
Aboard the boat were Bolan, Urbina, Ramona and
Rodriguez.

The boat skipper had been told by Iturbe that he
was to follow El Comandante's orders. He understood that this was an unsanctioned operation and that
he could get into big trouble. He'd also been told that
Octavo Marzo belonged to Fraternidad and that the
men on board were probably Fidelistos.

"Clever man, Jorge," he said to Bolan. "Every-
body with a reason to hate Fidel. Hmm? Every one of
us."

Bolan nodded. He wouldn't ask. He'd let Rodriguez tell him, if he wanted to, why he hated the Cuban Communists and their leader. But Rodriguez had
said all he wanted to say. He picked up a pair of sunglasses and shoved them into place on his nose. He'd
put aside his white nautical cap and now wore a big
straw hat with a floppy brim, which shaded his eyes
much better than the little cap.

"Some girl, that," Rodriguez said, glancing at Ramona, who sat in the fishing chair at the stern. "I
couldn't believe it when she deep-sixed that car. She
said it was hot. That doesn't mean—"

"She didn't steal it."

Bolan went down to the cabin to have a closer look
at the weapons Ramona had brought. There were four
assault rifles. Bolan was impressed by her choice and

wondered how many more of these the group ha[
since they cost more than two thousand dollars apiec[
The weapons were SG551s, manufactured by a Sw[
company named Schweizerische Industrie-Gesel[
schaft, better known as SIG. They fired 5.56 mm ar[
munition out of 30-round magazines at a rate of seve[
hundred shots per minute. The magazines were tran[
parent, allowing the shooter to check his ammo sit[
ation at a glance. The front sight was equipped with[
lighted night-sight—which might prove important.[

He'd checked out this rifle before, but until [
picked one up he'd forgotten how light it was. T[
stock, butt, grips and magazine were all made of [
rugged plastic.

Ramona had brought plenty of ammunition, and [
addition had brought two mini-Uzis and a dozen gr[
nades. She watched him examine the equipment, ar[
it was plain that she was waiting for his approval.

"Good stuff, Ramona," he said. "Do you ar[
Tomás know how to use these rifles?"

"I figured we'd have time to learn," she replied.

He climbed back up to the bridge.

"Quite an arsenal," Rodriguez commente[
"Doesn't look like you're planning on only *observi*[
that boat."

"I plan to observe it if we find it. But they might n[
like being observed."

"That's right. They don't. Fraternidad doesn't li[
it, and the Castro boats, they don't like it, either. Th[
can get pretty hard-nosed about it."

Bolan suspected he'd just heard the reason why Rodriguez detested Fraternidad and the Castro government. But once more the man elected not to say more.

The sun rose high over the blue-green water. Even with the ocean wind blowing briskly, the heat soon bore down, and the decks became hot to the touch.

Islamorada was a twin-diesel fisherman, a businesslike boat designed and built for one purpose—to take sport fishermen out to sea. It was narrow, with a sharp, high bow tapering back to a narrow stern. The cabin wasn't glassed in but solid-walled, with sturdy round portholes instead of picture windows. Appointments aboard were utilitarian. Its decks weren't teak, but painted oak. The three fishing chairs, one at the center of the stern, one to each side a little forward, were the one concession to luxury.

The boat was equipped with a depth sounder and with ship-to-shore radio, but not with radar. There was no galley. An ample supply of beer and soft drinks was stowed in a big ice chest inside the cabin, as well as sandwiches wrapped in aluminum foil. Another ice chest on the stern deck would have been stuffed with bait, but this wasn't a fishing trip and Rodriguez had brought no bait.

To their left as *Islamorada* forged southwest they were never out of sight of U.S. Highway 1, following the chain of keys and bridges and causeways to Key West. They could see the cars speeding by, and across the low keys they could spot white clouds lying on the Atlantic horizon.

A little more than four hours away from the dock Rodriguez turned the boat due south and passed under a bridge between two keys. On the open Atlantic seas rose higher. The wind was stiffer, and *Islamorada* began to climb and plunge.

Turning on a course down the outside of the Florida Keys, Rodriguez began to scan the sea through large binoculars. "Aha," he muttered after a moment. He handed the binoculars to Bolan. "So, did we make up the twenty miles, or not?"

Bolan saw what he meant. Half a mile farther out, fighting the seas as was *Islamorada,* was a handsome yacht. Through the binoculars the warrior could read the name *Octavo Marzo.*

Rodriguez eased back on the throttles. "Okay," he said. "Fish. They'll be looking at us, just as we're looking at them."

Leaving Bolan at the wheel, Rodriguez climbed down to the deck, strapped Ramona into the rear chair, put a pole in the socket and in her hands and began to trail an artificial lure. He put Urbina in the left seat and ran an outrigger to carry his line fifteen feet apart from hers.

"Want to fish, comandante?" he asked when he joined Bolan at the wheel.

"Somebody's got to play deckhand."

It was well he said so, because within ten minutes Ramona had a fish on the line, and he had to help her land a tough black bonito. They cut the hook and threw it back.

From inside the cabin he studied *Octavo Marzo* through binoculars. Most of its cabin space was glassed in, and it was obviously air-conditioned. Everything was polished brass and teak, gleaming in the sunlight. The big yacht caught up with *Islamorada* very slowly, and it was noon before it passed a little ahead.

By then Ramona had caught another bonito and Urbina a long mackerel. A shark cut the tail off the mackerel before they could haul it aboard.

Bolan couldn't see Gurza aboard *Octavo Marzo*. He did see ten or twelve hard-looking men, some of them drinking, some smoking cigars. He saw no sign of weapons, and no women. A dozen men out for a party cruise would surely have women aboard. The absence of women suggested a business trip.

"Are we going to lose her?" Bolan asked as he watched the yacht slowly edging farther and farther ahead.

Rodriguez shook his head. "She'll be going into Key West to refuel."

"What makes you think so?"

"Speed. She's kept up too much rpm all day to have enough left in his tanks to cross over into Cuban waters and come back. She's got to refuel. So do we."

"Think she'll lay over Key West overnight?"

"Depends on what she's doing. If she wants to reach Cuban waters in the dark, she'll move on out."

Islamorada caught up with *Octavo Marzo* as the big boat refueled. Rodriguez knew the boys on the dock at the marine service station and got his tanks pumped full very quickly. By the time the big yacht moved out of Key West, the little fisherman was ready to follow.

"They're going to figure this out sooner or later," Rodriguez said as he stood on the bridge, Bolan beside him, watching the yacht churn out of the harbor and into the hundred-mile-wide strait between Key West and the northern coast of Cuba. "She's fast. can't let her get too much ahead of us or we'll lose him."

"It's going to be dark as hell out there," Bolan said, knowing there wouldn't be a moon until well after midnight. "We run without lights—"

"She's got radar."

Bolan nodded and thought about that for a moment. "Maybe not. She's confounded the Coast Guard and even the Navy a dozen times. If her radar was querying, they'd detect that signal, wouldn't they? What do you want to bet she switches it off?"

"We've got no radar. If we run without radar..."

"We *watch*."

Holding throttles in and using fuel faster than he wanted to, Rodriguez kept the lights of *Octavo Marzo* in sight for the next three and a half hours. Bolan, Ramona and Urbina stood on the bridge and watched the sea with binoculars as the boat skipper ran without lights.

They passed uncomfortably close to a small rusty tub of a freighter whose dim lights they almost missed. Crewmen, cursing at them in Spanish, threw garbage at *Islamorada* but missed.

"Not too far off the coast of Cuba," Rodriguez said to Bolan. "Their patrol boats come out this far."

"Too close for comfort?"

"Nothing comfortable. Those hateful bastards!"

"You're taking a risk for yourself and your boat."

Rodriguez nodded. "I'll take it. Don't you worry why."

Night had settled in hard. They could see lights in the distance, nothing close except the running lights of the yacht, always a mile or so ahead. There wasn't much point now in scanning the sea with binoculars; except for running lights on boats that were showing them, they weren't going to see anything but murky night. From time to time Rodriguez pulled his throttles back to idle and listened.

"Look!" Ramona called.

Suddenly it was dark ahead. *Octavo Marzo* had gone dark.

"No goddamn radar," Rodriguez muttered, "and no goddamn moon."

"Why'd they turn off their lights?" Ramona asked.

"One of two reasons," Rodriguez replied. "They figured out we were back here, and following, or they don't want to be seen doing something good little boys aren't supposed to do."

With and without binoculars Bolan surveyed the sea ahead. *Octavo Marzo* hadn't slowed down. Rodriguez's throttles were in, and *Islamorada* struggled up waves and shot down their backsides. The fisherman strained to keep up with the big, fast yacht.

"Oh-oh," Urbina said abruptly. "Company."

No one needed to be told. Suddenly *Islamorada* was starkly lighted in a blinding glare.

"Are we still in international waters?" Bolan asked Rodriguez.

"For damn sure."

"Which means squat," Ramona said.

Rodriguez pulled back the throttles and brought his boat almost to a stop. "Take the wheel, comandante," he said grimly.

The skipper disappeared, and Bolan was left standing at the wheel. Out of the glare a voice through a bullhorn screamed in Spanish. Bolan couldn't make out more than a word or two. He checked the throttles. They were back as far as they could go. The boat wallowed.

"It's a Cuban patrol boat," Ramona said.

"I figured that."

"He says we're in Cuban waters, but he's lying."

"I figured that, too."

"Comandante, he's heavily armed. We can't—"

Without warning a streak of fire—the tail fire of a rocket—shot away from the stern deck of *Islamorada*. The trail of flame disappeared in a boiling red-and-yellow explosion, and the lights went out on the Cuban patrol boat.

A second streak flew into the flaming wreckage. In a quarter of a minute the patrol boat was gone, leaving nothing but smoking debris, with a little fire floating on the waves.

Rodriguez tossed the launching tubes overboard, then jumped up, grabbed the wheel and shoved in the throttles. "Ten Reds dead!" he yelled, "and before they could get radio word off! But we've got to get out of here!"

Ramona sat slumped on the bait box. "So much for *Octavo Marzo*," she said. "After seeing that, Gurza will—"

"Not necessarily," Bolan said. "At that distance he might have figured *we're* the ones blown up. Makes more sense. The patrol boat would be carrying heavy stuff. They wouldn't figure we are."

He stood scanning the sea through binoculars. The running lights on the yacht glowed, and it still kept to its same course, south, approaching Cuba's northern coast.

The Executioner returned to the bridge. Rodriguez had his throttles in, and *Islamorada* was surging east.

"South!" Bolan yelled, pointing at the receding lights of the yacht. "Don't lose him."

"Comandante, we've got to move out of here! When that patrol boat disappeared off their radar scopes—"

"Then get out of here south!"

Rodriguez considered for a moment, then spun his wheel.

"I think I'd turn on the running lights, too, Jesús," Bolan suggested.

"Why?"

"If I was in a Cuban patrol plane or chopper and spotted a boat running without lights, that's the one I'd report back to headquarters. When we're spotted from *Octavo Marzo,* they'll get very nervous about being tailed by an unlighted boat."

"Gotcha," Rodriguez said as he flipped the switches.

The yacht seemed to have slowed down—they were gaining on it.

"Jorge told me you carry heavy stuff aboard," Bolan said. "What you fired is heavier than anything I've got."

"I only had the two," Rodriguez replied. He turned and looked into Bolan's face, his own face hard and somber. "I can't risk being captured."

Bolan frowned. "A big problem?"

"A big problem. My grandfather, my father, my uncles, my brothers. There are three of us left. The family had eight of these boats, working out of Santiago. When Castro came to power, our boats were seized by waterfront bums. Most of them couldn't even get jobs hosing down boats that belonged to honorable men. But they were Fidelistos, and they had guns. Then we worked for them."

"I've heard the same story so many times," Bolan said, sympathetic to the man's loss.

"Only our story doesn't end quite the same way. The Rodriguezes have always been sailors, fishermen. We know the sea. We took three of our boats, brought our families aboard and escaped. Before we put out to sea we sank our other five boats, plus some others the Communists had stolen. Over the years—"

"A blood feud," Bolan concluded. "No quarter asked, none given."

"None asked, none given," Rodriguez repeated.

"*Octavo Marzo* isn't new to you," Bolan guessed.

"I've tailed him before. He's big and fast, and he's been searched many times. No cocaine, no heavy weapons."

"Then what's he doing?"

Rodriguez shrugged. "He takes rich men fishing."

Bolan studied the sea for a minute or so. "Jesús, you don't happen to have a rubber boat in the hold, do you?"

The man grinned. "Comandante, you don't think I'd bring people to sea without a lifeboat on board, do you?"

The yacht slowed and eventually almost stopped about twenty miles off Varadero. To the east, Rodriguez explained, lay a chain of islands and reefs, which were very tricky to navigate. The Florida Keys were a hundred and ten miles north. Havana was a hundred miles west.

Lights on the coast dimly defined the southern horizon. The navigation lights of aircraft blinked above the coastline—patrol planes, most likely.

Twice, while *Islamorada* was approaching the big yacht, a helicopter swept by overhead. Bolan guessed they were looking for the missing patrol boat.

Octavo Marzo ran slowly east, paralleling the coastline. Rodriguez, keeping half a mile or so north of it, passed the yacht and ran ahead. When he was a mile past the yacht, he cut south and crossed its projected course. This put his vessel between *Octavo Marzo* and the coastline. Rodriguez turned west and passed by the yacht, half a mile to its south.

Just as *Islamorada* had crossed the yacht's projected course, Bolan had dropped into the water in the rubber boat. He lay now in a gentle swell, crouched and occasionally stabbing the water with the paddle while the yacht bore down on him.

He wore a black wet suit and carried the Desert Eagle in its hip holster. Two grenades hung on his harness, and one of the SG551 assault rifles lay in the bottom of the raft.

The yacht was moving at idle speed, just fast enough to be sure the yacht would respond to its rudders. The Executioner paddled a little to the south. He wanted the yacht to pass him within twenty yards.

Except for the navigation lights, *Octavo Marzo* was showing no light. When it was very close, Bolan could see the weak light of the bridge instruments gleaming on the faces of two men.

Ashore, bright lights blinked—once, twice, three times, then a pause, then twice more. Maybe it was a signal. Maybe not.

The yacht passed him, no more than fifty feet away. Bolan lay in the bottom of the black rubber boat, unseen. The yacht continued on, but as slowly as it moved, he couldn't paddle fast enough to keep up with it.

It was turning. For a moment, as the man on the bridge throttled up one engine to make the turn sharper, the deep rumble of the diesel rolled across the water. Then, having reversed course, the man eased off the power again. *Octavo Marzo* would pass Bolan's rubber boat again, this time to the south, and this time maybe even closer.

The maneuver made sense. It was as if he were trolling for fish. But he wasn't, for damn sure.

Then, suddenly, a light flashed. This one was a signal, for sure, from another boat moving up from the coastline. A rendezvous.

Bolan paddled southward as hard as he could. He crossed *Octavo Marzo*'s course and stopped, keeping an eye out for the other boat.

And there it was. A rugged work boat, not very different from *Islamorada*.

The two pilots knew their routine. The yacht reversed engines and stopped, and the smaller boat maneuvered alongside. A man tossed a rope, and in a moment the two boats were lashed together, rising and falling in unison in an easy swell.

Men began to talk, but Bolan couldn't hear enough to know what was going on. But it was evident that they were transferring something from one boat to the other.

That occupied their attention. Fully. Quietly he paddled up to the south side of the second boat. He guessed there were three men on the second boat, and all of them would be on the side next to *Octavo Marzo*, wrestling crates. He couldn't see exactly what they were doing, but it monopolized their attention so completely that he was able to toss a loop over a cleat and lash the rubber boat to the Cuban boat.

Without raising his head too far, so as to be seen, Bolan watched the loading—*off* the big yacht and onto the Cuban boat. It made sense. The narcs and Coast Guard searched the yacht when it came back into Florida waters, and they didn't find any drugs. Because *Octavo Marzo* was being used to carry something *to* Cuba, not to bring something back.

The transfer didn't take long. The crates appeared to be heavy, but there weren't many of them. The two boats separated, the Cuban vessel turning south, going home, the *Octavo Marzo* turning north.

Bolan, crouched in the rubber raft, was being towed south into Cuban waters—into waters where Rodriguez couldn't bring his boat. The warrior knew he had very little time to do whatever he was going to do.

He raised his head over the gunwale and risked a look. If there were three men on board—and he thought he had judged that right—two of them had gone below. One man was on the bridge. The air smelled strongly of cigar smoke, and the man on the bridge wasn't smoking. The smell was coming out through the gangway. At least one of the other men was below.

With throttles maybe halfway advanced, the boat's diesels were rumbling, and the propellers were churning up a froth behind. The noise level was high enough to cover a quiet boarding.

The warrior heaved himself over the gunwale and onto the stern. He crouched and waited. Nothing. So far no one had noticed him.

His knife was a Bali-Song, a top-quality professional soldier's blade contained inside rotating, fold-out twin handles that could themselves be used as lethal cudgels. The stainless-steel blade was as strong as anything he'd ever seen in a knife. He shoved it under the lid of one of the crates and pried upward. Nails resisted, but he twisted the knife and the board rose. The nails squeaked as they pulled out of wood, but they gave.

Bolan pried off another board and checked inside the crate. He lifted out one of the heavy white paperboard cartons inside and read the words on the box.

Now the whole thing made sense. All of it. He dropped the carton into the rubber boat, threw himself over the side and into the boat and cut the rope. The Cuban boat churned on south, leaving the black rubber boat floating on the sea alone. Bolan waited five minutes before he took out his flashlight and risked a signal to *Islamorada*.

7

Bolan cut open the white carton and spread its contents on top of the bait box. Ramona shone a flashlight on the heavily wrapped plastic package. "Computer chips..." she muttered.

"I don't get it," Urbina said. "Not exactly."

"Technology," Bolan told him. "Embargoed technology. Maybe the other cartons held other items. Installed in a computer one of those chips can—"

"Guide a missile to a target," Ramona finished.

"Right. And a lot of other things. For example, computer chips are the brains of a lot of heavy-duty military hardware. Nations that have the best computer chips have a huge advantage in all kinds of fields. The U.S. and Japan manufacture the most sophisticated chips, and we have a strict embargo on exporting them to countries like Castro's Cuba. The Japanese cooperate. The world's dictators will pay practically anything for state-of-the-art chips."

Rodriguez pointed toward the lights of *Octavo Marzo,* still visible on the stern of the yacht, now more than a mile north of them. "What do you suppose they paid?"

"Whatever it was, it wasn't cocaine. They wouldn't take a chance hauling that stuff. My guess is Cuba pays in credits, bank deposits. And I'd guess Frater-nidad gets paid in advance.''

Rodriguez stood erect and looked around. He could see the lights on twenty boats, maybe forty; this was a heavy-traffic area. "That patrol boat. Are you call-ing it a coincidence?"

Bolan shook his head. "I'd call it a boat assigned to make sure nobody got too close to the yacht when they were making the transfer.''

"They lost it, and they know it. So where are their compatriots? They should be looking for us.''

"They're out there," Bolan said, looking around, "checking boats. But which boat do they look at first?''

"The one that moves north," Rodriguez replied.

"So we watch out.''

"Or we don't move north," Ramona stated. "If we don't follow the yacht—''

"Never mind that," Rodriguez growled. "I want that son of a bitch.''

Ramona nodded. "North no matter what, then.''

For the next two hours they remained on high alert. All four of them stayed on the bridge or on deck, watching the sea, looking for the heavily armed boat that, this time, would probably shoot before it asked questions. But no such boat came. *Octavo Marzo* stayed a mile ahead of them, its diesels churning up a little less than maximum speed.

The hours passed slowly. When morning broke, *Is-lamorada* was struggling through surging seas, en-gines alternately roaring and purring.

Bolan climbed to the bridge, followed by Ramona. Urbina was asleep on the bench behind the wheel, unconscious of the salt spray that fell on him as the boat climbed a wave, then plunged. Rodriguez stood at the wheel.

While Bolan and Ramona had slept, *Islamorada* had gained on the yacht, which was only a quarter of a mile head, looking as big as a battleship.

"They got it figured out," Rodriguez said. "They know we're following them."

"I thought they were faster," Bolan commented.

"Not in these seas. This old tub is built to run in this kind of weather. The yacht..." He shook his head. "It wasn't built to run fast when seas are high. It was built to weather it out, not to disturb the rich people on board."

Bolan shoved his cap down low to keep the spray out of his eyes. "Where are we?"

"Precisely? I figure twenty-four degrees, thirty minutes north, eighty degrees, forty minutes west. That puts us on a course directly back to Miami, or Key Largo, anyway, with no refueling stop at Key West. She can do it, probably. We'll have to go in on one of the keys, Key Largo maybe."

"What makes you say they know we're following them?"

"They're watching us all the time with binoculars. We're making them nervous."

Bolan raised his binoculars and had a look. It was true. Men were watching them from the stern. "How long before we catch up?"

"Give me another hour and we'll be running in their wake."

"And do what?" Ramona asked.

Rodriguez turned to Bolan. "Comandante?"

"We'll see what happens," Bolan said. "See what *they* do."

The Executioner wondered what firepower Fraternidad had aboard the yacht. If they had anything comparable to what Rodriguez had fired at the Cuban patrol boat the previous night, *Islamorada* was in big trouble.

He doubted they did. *Octavo Marzo* had been searched, and nothing like missile launchers had been found. The yacht was a smuggler, not a fighter. Illegal cargo would be dumped. On the other hand, with hardguys aboard, they wouldn't go defenseless.

Bolan talked to Rodriguez. They agreed. With Ramona at the wheel and Urbina sleeping, the two men carried the bait box up to the bridge. They set it out ahead of the wheel and other controls, on the cabin roof, and filled it with hard objects—the boat's anchors, a spare propeller, two fuel cans filled with water, big fishing reels, cans of soda and beer, then tarps and blankets—anything that would serve to stop bullets.

"They're watching you," Ramona said, staring at the yacht through the binoculars. "They've got the idea and know what's coming."

"*We* don't know what's coming," Bolan replied.

That was a fact. Should he order this little group, on this little boat, to attack the big yacht?

But he didn't have to make a decision. At mid-morning, while the wind was even higher and the two boats were struggling against the seas, the decision was taken out of his hands.

"Comandante . . ." Ramona said cautiously, pointing toward the sky to the north and raising her binoculars to look.

Bolan saw what she meant and raised his own. A twin-engine plane was approaching. It flew at no more than two thousand feet above the water on a steady course. The aircraft buzzed over the yacht and then, a second later, over the fishing boat.

"I think we've got trouble," Bolan said. He grabbed for a SG551 and crouched on the deck of the bridge, behind Rodriguez. "Below!" he yelled at Urbina and Ramona.

The young man leaped from the bridge as the airplane circled to the east and turned into a course to bring it directly over *Islamorada*. Ramona grabbed an SG551 and crouched beside Bolan.

The plane came in. "Don't fire on it," Bolan ordered. "It might not be what we think."

If it was what they thought, the pilot had made a mistake—which Bolan saw. A plane like that wasn't equipped with forward-firing machine guns. If men on board were to fire on the fishing boat, the plane had to pass a little to one side, so they could shoot from the windows.

Maybe it was only an observation aircraft. The DEA flew planes like that. Bolan put a hand on Ramona's arm and restrained her from lifting the assault rifle as the plane swept overhead.

But this plane swept into a wide turn and came back from the west. This time it would pass to the north.

"Not until they fire," Bolan said grimly.

He knew there was no point in telling Ramona to go below. Urbina obeyed orders. She didn't.

Rodriguez dropped to his knees behind the wheel to accept the protection of the bait box if the airplane was hostile.

It was. It passed above at no more than five hundred feet, less than fifteen hundred feet to the north of the boat. Bolan watched through his binoculars.

The windows were open. You couldn't open the windows on a plane like that, which meant they'd been knocked out. He could see gun muzzles.

Suddenly slugs began to chop the water, all around, but none hit the boat. Firing from a plane like that, only an experienced gunman would be able to hit anything.

But they'd keep trying.

"No quarter this time, comandante." Rodriguez bent down and picked up another SG551. "Tomás!" he called.

Bolan nodded. "No quarter."

Urbina came up from below, carrying his own assault rifle.

As they watched the airplane sweep in, splinters flew from the bait box and the bridge rail.

"From *Octavo Marzo!*" Rodriguez yelled.

"Never mind the yacht for now!" Bolan ordered. "Take the plane first!"

The airplane was off their bow, at an angle. The Executioner fired a burst from the SG551, the others

joining in a heartbeat later. Someone scored a hit
Chunks of metal and other debris were torn off th·
aircraft and fell into the sea.

The pilot banked abruptly, frightened, apparently
by the slugs chopping his airplane to pieces. The ma·
neuver made it impossible for his gunmen to fire o·
the fishing boat. As well, he presented the belly of th·
aircraft as a target to the four gunners on the boat
who opened up simultaneously.

The airplane continued its steep, banked turn, the·
roared around and lost altitude until it cartwheele·
into the ocean.

"Yes!" Rodriguez shouted. "Now *that* son of
bitch!" He rammed another magazine into his rifl·
and fired on *Octavo Marzo*.

Gunmen on the stern of the yacht had continued t
fire on *Islamorada*. The bait box was shot full o·
holes, and the wood around the bridge was splin·
tered. Some of the hardguys had decided a better ide·
was to lower their sights and fire on the hull of th·
pursuing fisherman.

"We've got to stop that," Bolan gritted.

He was a marksman, and the SG551s were equippe·
with excellent diopter sights. He rested the rifle on th·
rail of the bridge and let loose a shot toward the ster·
of the yacht. The round blew a shower of splinters o·
the teak rail and dropped one gunman. His secon·
shot staggered another gunner, who leaped up, stun·
bled back and fell to the deck.

"Tomás," Bolan called.

"Comandante."

"Bring me up the Uzis."

Urbina crawled backward, dropped to the lower deck and went below. A moment later he returned, carrying the two mini-Uzis Ramona had brought from the swamp arsenal, plus extra magazines.

"Time to put a stop to this," Bolan said. "I like the chopping power of these Uzis better than the precise bursts you can get from the SGs. Hold her steady, Jesús."

They were now less than a hundred yards behind *Octavo Marzo*. It was a long shot for a machine pistol, but the warrior had done it before. He knelt on the pitching deck, resting his arms and the Uzi on the bridge rail. He judged the rising and falling of the two boats and fired a short burst.

The slugs blew a hole in the stern, but he didn't know what it had done inside. He waited, aimed and fired a second burst. The steering mechanism, the fuel tanks, the engines themselves—all were within the range of a storm of slugs blasting through the stern.

While he was reloading the mini-Uzi, Ramona and Urbina fired bursts of 5.56 mm slugs through the rear doors of the main cabin of the yacht, glass and wood shooting into the air.

"Comandante..."

Bolan saw what Rodriguez meant to bring to his attention. *Octavo Marzo* was slowing. The froth churned up behind its propellers was only half of what it had been.

"What are we going to do?" Ramona asked.

"What do you want to do?" Bolan asked.

"Sink it."

"That might not be easy."

"What is?"

The warrior directed Rodriguez to bring the boat t
the right, then to advance throttles and bring the boa
up on the right of the yacht. So far they'd fired into it
stern. Now they'd move alongside and fire into i
broadside.

Guns cracked from the rear deck and the ope
bridge of the yacht. There had been about a doze
gunners aboard the vessel, less than ten of them sti
effective. They might not have weapons as good a
Bolan's team had, but they began to pour a sustaine
torrent of fire into the fishing boat. At fifty yards thei
fire was inaccurate, but slugs chopped through th
gunwales and into the hull of the fishing boat. Soone
or later they were going to hit somebody.

Rodriguez stood at the wheel, keeping his craf
parallel and at the fifty-yard range.

"Cut across his bow," Bolan told Rodriguez.

The man smiled wryly as he nodded acknowledg
ment.

Gunners on the yacht began to smash out the win
dows of the main cabin so that they could fire fror
inside. Bolan and Urbina directed their gunfire ac
cordingly.

As he came around to cut across the bow of th
yacht, Rodriguez allowed the range between the tw
boats to diminish. Fire from the bigger vessel wasn'
as heavy as it had been; but now, at closer range, i
became more deadly. A pistol slug struck the com
pass just in front of Rodriguez and showered him wit
glass that gashed his face.

Then Urbina was hit. He cried out and staggered across the rear deck, clutching his leg above the knee.

Bolan jumped down from the bridge, ran inside the cabin and returned with the canvas bag that held the grenades.

It was a long throw. His first grenade struck the hull of the yacht and fell into the water, where it went off and threw up a geyser of saltwater.

The gunmen saw what Bolan was doing and concentrated their fire on him. Rodriguez let go of the wheel, grabbed the mini-Uzi that lay on the deck of the bridge and swept the main cabin of the yacht with slugs until his magazine ran dry.

Ramona, too, fired bursts into the main cabin. She used up her ammo and snatched up the SG551 that Urbina had dropped.

Bolan pitched another grenade, which hit the forward deck, rolled across and exploded, blasting a storm of lethal steel pellets through the forward windows.

The big yacht was quiet now, rolling gently on the waves. It was taking on water through the holes Ramona had blown in the hull.

"We've got to take the survivors aboard," Bolan said.

"The hell with them," Ramona snarled. She was staring at Urbina, who sat on the deck clutching his bleeding leg, gritting his teeth in pain. "Let them drown."

Bolan shook his head. "No way. We don't let wounded men drown. There's a first-aid kit in my gear that Jorge brought to the dock. Do what you can for Tomás. Jesús, do you have a bullhorn on board?"

Rodriguez shook his head.

Bolan stood at the rail and yelled, "We'll take you on board! Throw down your guns and come out. Bring out the wounded."

Rodriguez began to edge his boat closer to *Octavo Marzo*.

Bolan yelled again. "Come out on the rear! Now!"

A burst from a machine pistol erupted through one of the broken windows on the yacht. It drilled through the cabin, barely missing Ramona.

Rodriguez jammed his throttles in and spun his wheel, turning the stern toward the yacht.

Bolan pitched another grenade, which landed on the roof of the main cabin. The explosion blew a jagged hole in the roof, and the pellets shot into the cabin.

The range between the two boats opened rapidly. Soon *Islamorada* was fifty yards, then a hundred yards away. As Bolan stood watching, a wave rolled over the stern of the yacht, which took on water and began to settle deeper.

"Jesús—"

"Forget it, man." He spun the wheel and turned on a northerly course.

The fishing boat was damaged. Urbina's wound wasn't threatening, either to his life or his leg, but it was painful; he lost a lot of blood and needed medical attention.

They were reluctant, even so, to take the boat and the wounded young man into a port where they'd have to answer questions. Rodriguez had a solution to that.

He knew the area very well, and he knew where to find a private cove and a discreet doctor. Running as fast as he dared with what fuel he had left, he reached the Keys in three hours. Crossing under a bridge, he entered Florida Bay. Half an hour later he brought *Islamorada* to a rickety wooden dock on a sandy island.

The man at the fuel pump greeted him with effusive warmth, then frowned over the bullet damage to the boat. "I see y'all want more than fuel. Wondered why y'all come t' see *me,* Jesús."

"We need to see Doc Gainer," Rodriguez said quietly.

"Okay. Put your man in my pickup. Doc's home, I think."

Two hours later they were on their way north toward Homestead and Miami, riding in Doc Gainer's huge old Cadillac. Rodriguez drove. He'd take Bolan, Ramona and Urbina to Miami, then return to where his friend was repairing the damage to *Islamorada*.

Ramona asked Rodriguez to pull into a gas station in Homestead to let her make a telephone call. Minutes later she returned, tears streaming down her face.

"Jorge Iturbe..." she whispered. "Jorge is dead. They killed him."

8

They sat in the screened-in room in the swamp, and Alvarado told them about Jorge Iturbe's death.

"A bomb...about noon. Somebody walked up to his house and threw a bomb through the window into the kitchen where he was having lunch with his wife. He'd just gone home for lunch. Both were killed. His two little girls were in school, thank God."

Urbina lay on a cot Ramona had set up in a corner of the room. Sedated, he slept restlessly, slipping in and out of consciousness.

Ramona sat wearily slumped in a chair. She wore camouflage fatigue pants and a white T-shirt, both damp with sweat. "What we did last night was so great," she murmured sadly. "Then this."

The warrior had to admit he was tired, and he wondered how he would fight this war without the help of the man who knew the territory and the players. These kids were brave, but Iturbe had been the seasoned veteran they needed.

The detective's wife had been an innocent. War without quarter, Rodriguez had said. So be it.

IN A GUARDED penthouse suite high above Collins Avenue in Miami Beach, Virgilio Gurza, too, was declaring war without quarter.

"The yacht!" he screamed. "And four of my men! Not to mention the three others shot up so bad they might never be whole again! Never mind the half a million worth of computer chips."

"Worse than that," Manuel Castillo said. "The theft of those chips—a whole box of them, right out from under our noses—means our cover is blown and the deal's been busted. Now somebody knows."

In complete contrast to the heavy-bellied Gurza, Castillo was a thin man, dressed in a handsomely tailored gray suit. In fact, he looked as if he belonged in this luxurious suite, which Gurza definitely didn't. Castillo's hair was silver, but his thick eyebrows were black. His nose was thin and pointed, as was his chin. He stood at the window, looking out at the beach and the Atlantic, a man whose very bearing spoke of self-confidence and authority.

Gurza puffed on a fat cigar. "What can they prove?" he grunted.

"They don't have to prove anything. All they have to do is know. It was a sweet deal, Virgilio, but this breaks it."

"It doesn't have to."

"It's already broken," Castillo replied calmly and smoothly. "Colonel Sierra sent me to tell you that."

Gurza frowned as he stared through his cigar smoke at the man. Castillo was a captain in Dirección General de Inteligencia, better known as the DGI, the Cuban secret service. The DGI had been organized and trained by the KGB, and even when the character of the KGB changed in Russia, the character of the secret service in Cuba didn't change. Fidel still clung to orthodox Marxism-Leninism.

In his mind Gurza reviewed the role the DGI had played in the deal, trying to figure if there was any way he could work it without them.

No way. Their agents stole the chips and other computer parts from high-tech companies in Texas and California. They hired the hoodlums who took items off the loading docks by hijacking trucks, sometimes actually by taking the stuff off the factory floor with the cooperation of corrupt employees. There was a market for the chips in the States, but the real money was in exporting it in violation of the embargo. That had been Gurza's part of the deal. Using his yacht and other boats, he'd been hauling the contraband down to the northern coast of Cuba and transferring it to Cuban boats. The narcs always figured he was importing cocaine, never guessing he was exporting technology.

The Cuban government, in turn, sold most of the chips and other technology to China, North Korea, Libya, Syria, Iraq or whoever desperately wanted the stuff and couldn't get it the legal way. There was a huge profit for the Cuban government, which was always short of hard currency and needed it to fund subversion in the countries around the Caribbean. For Fraternidad there had been less profit but still a lot of money. Some of it came to Gurza in cash; some of it in white powder.

No, he couldn't do it without the DGI, and if Colonel Ernesto Sierra was pulling the DGI out, the deal was dead. It *was* dead. Sierra had sent his chief man in the States to say so.

Gurza sighed loudly, unhappily. "I want the ass of the guy who broke the deal."

"Colonel Sierra is interested in him, as well. I brought two boys with me. If anybody can take out this invincible man, they can. They've handled some important jobs. Colonel Sierra has put out a half-million-dollar contract on this guy. He expects you to match that money. These boys would love to have that million. They can retire on it. Or so can anybody else who does the job."

"Yeah? Well, where are we going to find the son of a bitch?"

Castillo turned away from the window, walked to a cabinet and picked up a bottle of cognac. He poured himself a drink. "We don't have to find him. He's going to come looking for... Well, for you, actually. And that's when we get him."

"Why's he coming looking for me?"

"He thinks you took out Detective Sergeant Jorge Iturbe," Castillo replied. He raised the snifter and sipped brandy. "In fact, I imagine everyone thinks you took out the detective."

"What? Are you making me bait in a trap?"

Castillo smiled. "When he comes to get the guy he thinks killed the cop, he'll find a little surprise waiting for him."

BOLAN STOOD watching the swamp. He'd figured ou
that there were just four young cubanos out in th
swamp, around the clearing and this building. At leas
one man was awake all night, patrolling the area and
keeping watch, particularly on the road.

Homero Alvarado wasn't one of them. He'd left the
night before. Bolan hadn't asked where he was going
assuming the youth was going home. But he was bac
now. He'd left his car outside the gate and was walk
ing toward the clearing. He carried two big brown bag
of groceries, and newspapers were stuffed in one of the
bags.

"Two big news stories," he said. "One about Jorge
and his wife and one about *Octavo Marzo*. Member
of Fraternidad who were picked up in rubber boats say
they were attacked by a Cuban patrol boat. Nobod
believes them."

"I suppose they've got no suspects in Jorge's mur
der?" Bolan asked.

"No."

"So what do we do?" Ramona queried.

"We've done a great deal already," Alvarado re
plied. "That is, El Comandante has done a great deal
Gurza is so afraid he's left his home. Angeles is—
Well, Angeles is in the hospital. The yacht is at th
bottom of the ocean. And—"

"And Jorge is dead," Ramona concluded bitterly.

"Comandante," Urbina said weakly from the cot
"what do we do?"

"We keep doing what we've been doing. I've used
the technique many times before. We keep hitting

1em where it hurts, make them angry and wait for 1em to make a big mistake."

"I know where to hit them next," Urbina announced.

LVARADO UNDERSTOOD what his companion had old Bolan. He could take the warrior to the next target.

"It's a soft probe," the warrior had said to Ramona. "A one-man job. You can't go with me."

Alvarado could, and the first thing they did was rop off his car and rent a different one. Then, following the young man's directions, Bolan drove into 1e southwest quarter of the city, into an area west of Coral Gables that was a big cubano community.

Alvarado had explained it before, and Ramona and rbina had confirmed what he'd said. As Marxism 1st its credibility in the world, its hard-liners re-eated—to Beijing, many of them, to Albania, to uba. But what good were they there? They dis-ersed. They went out into the world again, to where 1ey might be able to keep alive the old Cold War line f communism.

"And some of them are here," Alvarado had said. They have a...what would you call it? A cell? Yeah, Communist cell. They call themselves Brigada Popul-lar—the Popular Brigade. They're just one cell. here are others here in Miami. Fraternidad is afraid f them—not because there are so many, but because 1ey're fanatics. They're true believers. To them Che iuevara was a hero. Castro, Stalin, Beria, even. Now,

well, many of them are fugitives. Fugitives from ju
revenge."

The cell had established a headquarters, he'd co
cluded, in the district they were driving through.

The building the young man pointed out was an ol
automobile agency, tightly boarded up. To the wa
rior, the fact that it was so secure was suspicious. A
they drove by he noticed that the coverings over the b
windows weren't just scrap lumber put up to repla
broken glass—they were solid lumber, carefully fitt
into place as if to fortify the building. The entries h
been replaced by steel doors without windows.

"What do you suppose the police think this is?
Bolan asked.

"It's a liquor warehouse. It really is. There a
hundreds of cases of liquor stored inside, but th
leaves plenty of room for what the Brigade uses t
building for."

"Which is?"

"To store weapons and explosives. Jorge knew
He wanted the police to raid the place, but th
couldn't until they got enough evidence to get a wa
rant."

"I don't need a warrant."

SOFT PROBE. Bolan ordered Alvarado to take a sto
at the counter and near the window in a bakery dow
the street, where he could drink coffee and watch. Fo
himself, the warrior meant to have a closer look at th
so-called liquor warehouse.

As a former auto agency, the building was on
corner, separated from the streets by broad blackto

arking lots. A few cars sat on the lots, all but two of them disabled and sitting on flat tires. The building had been constructed of concrete block and covered with white stucco, which was falling off. Of the doors into the building, all were permanently sealed but two: the front door and a big loading door on one side. Graffiti smeared the wooden barricades on the windows.

To a seasoned observer there was something conspicuously phony about the whole layout. The building was supposed to look run-down, shabby, all but abandoned. But the air-conditioning machinery on the roof was running hard. The graffiti were nothing but random swirls of paint, not the letters and designs that characterized the real thing. The disabled cars in the parking lot weren't worthless wrecks, but just old cars with flat tires. Each looked to Bolan as if it could be started and driven off if someone just pumped up the tires.

The warrior had long experience about what to look for when probing a position. Standing across the street, he watched the wind blow paper litter across the parking lots. Odd. In the first place, this wasn't a neighborhood where litter was thrown on the street. It seemed as if the paper on these lots had been purposefully scattered there as part of the camouflage.

Something else. When gusts lifted paper, they lifted dust—they lifted dust on the street, on the sidewalks, on the lots. But some of the dust on the parking lots—thick dust, a coating of it—didn't move.

Bolan walked around the block and returned, this time on the side of the street beside the building, di-

rectly past it, close. That dust... Yeah, the win
couldn't move it. It was cemented down, and it co
ered something. Wires. Every one of those suppo
edly disabled cars was connected to the building by
pair of wires.

Why? Alarm sensors, meant to detect intruders :
the parking lot? Hardly likely. Sensors on the buil
ing itself could do that. No, more likely they we
wired with explosives. In case of a police raid the ca
would explode, throwing fire and shrapnel, creatin
the confusion the terrorists inside would use to cov
their escape.

This old car agency building, right inside the city
Miami, was a fort. The wooden covers on the wi
dows were backed by sheets of steel. When Bolan g
close, he could see through the cracks to the steel.

The neighbors had moved away. For half a block
every direction the little buildings were vacant. Pe
ple were afraid of this place. Afraid to complain, to
more than likely.

Bolan crossed the street and stood in the sun o
posite the building, completing his probe and thin
ing about how to attack. As he stood there, the b
doors opened and a truck came out. The sign paint
on the truck read Cardenas Espiritosas—Carden
Liquors.

For a minute the door was open, and the warri
had a look inside the former automobile agency.
was, in fact, a warehouse for liquor. The interior
the building was brightly lighted by banks of fluore
cent tubes. The stacks of cartons of liquor were clear

visible from the streets, together with a forklift used to move pallets.

The men inside were young and muscular—fighting men, from the look of them. He saw no weapons. They wouldn't be careless enough to let weapons be seen from the street.

"You looking for something, *anglo?*" asked a man who'd left one of the vacant buildings and approached Bolan almost unnoticed. The young man spoke with a heavy Spanish accent. "You got business here?"

Bolan turned and saw that he was facing a tough, menacing young man in blue jeans whose nylon jacket undoubtedly concealed a weapon.

The Executioner shrugged. Maybe he could rid himself of this guy by being casual. "My business is insurance. I was wondering who owns that building and if—"

"If your business is insurance, go mind your business," the hardguy growled.

Bolan shrugged again. "Okay..."

The warrior turned to walk away, but abruptly the young man stepped in front of him with a switchblade in his hand. "Just a minute. You don't walk away from me till I say you can."

A quick chop on the wrist knocked the knife loose, and a fist to the belly doubled the tough guy over. Bolan grabbed him and jerked the punk's arm up behind, forcing him to rise on the tips of his toes to avoid dislocation of his shoulder. The warrior reached around, found the pistol hidden under the nylon jacket and pulled it out. He gave the man a shove, and the guy staggered forward.

The pistol was a Soviet-made Tokarev TT-33. Bolan had been seeing them for years, and the fact that this guy was carrying one was pretty strong evidence of who he was. He jerked out the magazine and pulled back the slide to eject the cartridge from the chamber. Then the Executioner tossed the pistol to the guy, but the young man was nursing a throbbing arm and didn't catch it. The Tokarev fell to the sidewalk.

"I know who you are," the young man muttered.

"Who am I?" Bolan asked.

"Whatever they call you. Different things. You're an enemy of the people."

"Why don't you get a new line? 'Enemy of the people' is out of style. *You're* out of style. Your kind. You talk about the people. Well, you don't fool them anymore."

The young man smiled crookedly, showing bad teeth. "We'll see. *You* may be invincible, but the rotten way of life you represent isn't."

"Okay. You want to carry a warning to your friends across the street? Tell them the next time I come by here I want to see the doors wide open, the windows uncovered and the place abandoned. I want to see cops hauling out what you've got over there. Tell them they don't have much time."

"You're crazy."

"Just carry the warning. It's the only one they're going to get."

"TONIGHT?" Alvarado asked skeptically.

"Tonight," Bolan replied.

"Alone?"

"Alone."

The young man sighed. "As you say, comandante. Jorge told us to do it your way."

"Alone except for one element of it. I want you to drive me, then I want you to stay away. I mean away, Homero. And I want you to help me keep Ramona from trying to mix herself up in it."

"Jorge also told us to help you."

"Tonight it's a one-man job," Bolan said firmly. "And you will help me. I want you to help me select what I need out of your arsenal and load it in the car—late and quiet when Ramona is asleep. Got it?"

Alvarado nodded.

"Tomás and Ramona were a big help when we went after *Octavo Marzo*. Tonight I'd only have to worry about keeping her, or you, from getting hurt. Tomorrow? Well, tomorrow, we'll see."

"As you say."

NOT UNTIL WELL after midnight did Bolan get up from the sleeping bag and slip out of the screened-in room to meet Alvarado in the clearing. They traveled through the swamp to the arsenal building accompanied by two young cubanos who led the way.

Bolan had surveyed the cache of weapons but hadn't really taken inventory. Tonight he was going to need something very special.

Some of the weapons were left over from the 1960s when Cuban refugees had still hoped to invade Cuba from Florida bases. There were a hundred or so M-3 grease guns of World War II vintage, still in the original crates and packed in Cosmoline. He saw stacks of crates containing M-16s. They had no more than twenty or so of the SG551s Ramona had chosen for their attack on *Octavo Marzo*.

Stacked on a table in a corner were what Bolan wanted for the hit. They had only six of them, but they had plenty of extra magazines and a good supply of the .45 ammo required by the Ingram MAC-10, a powerful submachine gun equipped with a sound suppressor.

The Ingram could deliver devastating bursts of heavy slugs in close-range fighting. With the MAC sound suppressor attached, it wouldn't terrify the entire neighborhood with a deafening roar. The warrior unpacked an Ingram and hefted it. It was a competent, reliable weapon, perfect for fighting inside the warehouse—if he ever got in.

But how to accomplish that?

They had grenades and a supply of plastic explosive, but he saw nothing he could use to effect entry to that heavily fortified building.

"Comandante, have you seen these?"

Almost timidly Alvarado showed him a crate packed with ten Armbrusts.

The warrior wondered how they'd managed to get their hands on them. Armbrusts were shoulder-fired antitank missile launchers, a modern version of the old bazooka American troops had used against Panzers during World War II.

Like the Ingram, the Armbrust was the perfect weapon for the operation he was planning for tonight. It fired silently, making no smoke or flash to betray the position of the man firing it. But it could stop a tank, and it could blow open one of those steel-reinforced doors or windows.

Each Armbrust fired once only and was then tossed away. He took three of them.

With the cubano's help he loaded the Ingram and its extra magazines, and the Armbrusts, into the rental car. He took two grenades also—just two because they had to hang on his harness; he had quite enough to carry without any extra grenades.

He dressed in a set of the camouflage fatigues the cubanos had in ample supply, then donned the harness that carried the holster for the Desert Eagle, his Bali-Song knife and the leather pouches that held a flashlight and other equipment.

A little after 1:00 a.m. Alvarado drove toward Miami. "I looked in to see if Ramona was still asleep, comandante."

"Was she?"

"No. She wasn't there."

9

"I've got to change your assignment just a little, Homero," Bolan said when they were two blocks from the liquor warehouse. "After you fire an Armbrust, you throw it away. I want you to carry the empty tubes back to the car. I don't want to leave them lying on the street. I'm not sure how the Miami police will like our bringing antitank missiles into the city."

Alvarado nodded.

"I don't want you getting into the battle," Bolan continued. "After you pick up the tubes, you go. Understand?"

"I understand, comandante."

"Are you carrying a pistol?"

The young man nodded again and opened his jacket to show Bolan that he was carrying a Beretta 92-F.

"Use it if you have to. These guys will shoot first and ask questions later."

They left the car two blocks from the fortified warehouse, on another street, out of sight. Alvarado carried two of the Armbrusts. Bolan carried the third one, plus the Ingram submachine gun.

The sky was overcast. There was no moon, but the lights of the city were reflected from the low-lying cloud cover: a reddish light that cast no shadows. A little rain had fallen early in the evening. Most of the water had evaporated, but there were still shiny wet patches on the streets and sidewalks.

A hooker was working the street across from the warehouse. She wore a yellow nylon jacket, maybe against the rain that had fallen earlier, and tight, skimpy red shorts. She strolled toward Bolan and Alvarado, but didn't see them because they were in the shadow of a building. Then she turned and strolled the other way.

"She couldn't do any business out here at this hour," Bolan said. "She's a lookout."

"No, comandante. It's Ramona."

"Damn!"

When she turned again and walked toward them, Bolan stepped out of the shadow and beckoned to her. She sauntered slowly toward him, playing her role.

"What are you doing here?" he demanded.

Ramona shrugged. "It's my fight, not just yours."

"Suppose I tell you that you do more harm than good by being here."

"Suppose I tell you I don't believe it."

"I can't do what I have to do if I also have to watch out for you."

"Then *don't* watch out for me," she snapped.

Bolan stared past her toward the warehouse as he decided what to do about her. "Will you take orders?" he asked her without looking at her.

"Any except to go away."

"Did you bring a rifle or a machine pistol?"

"I've got a couple of Uzis in the pickup, which is what I drove here. It's parked around the corner."

"All right," he said. "I want you to stay out here and back me up. That's all you can do. It's possible that when I make my move, reinforcements will come in from somewhere. I don't know if you can stop them. I'll leave you the grenades, too. Homero—"

"I'll stay with Ramona, comandante."

"I don't want you two getting yourselves killed. Or hurt. You stay across the street, no matter what. If I don't come back, leave. No matter what happens, don't come across the street. Those are your orders." He stared hard at Ramona.

She faced him squarely, her eyes meeting his. "I'll follow those orders."

"All right. You two go get your Uzis. Stay in the shadows and don't be seen. If anybody tries to stop you, shoot."

In the hours before midnight the warrior had formed in his mind a plan of attack. Now that he was here, it looked good. It involved a diversion, then a frontal assault. Or maybe two diversions followed by an assault, depending on how things worked out.

He studied the position again while he waited for his two companions to return. Everything was just as he'd remembered it. Years of soft probes and recons had accustomed the warrior to gathering intel and absorbing the details of a situation with complete accuracy.

Alvarado and Ramona returned, and he briefed them quickly, then moved out. He carried one Armbrust and the MAC-10. His recon in the afternoon had shown him the way to make an approach to the warehouse without showing himself to the sentries who probably watched from the roof. He circled the block, keeping in the shadows. The approach he'd identified involved a walk between a house and a florist shop, both abandoned as was everything within half a block of what the nearby community recognized as a headquarters of the Brigada Popular.

Ever alert, he spotted danger. He wasn't the only one who could do a recon and identify approaches to the warehouse. A man stood ahead of him in the narrow passage between the vacant house and florist shop. They'd figured it out, too, and had posted a guard in this passage.

The man was a sentry, for sure, not just some drunk who'd stepped off the street to urinate or throw up. He cradled a deadly assault rifle. Bolan wasn't sure of the model, seeing only a profile in shadow, but it had the look of a Chinese-made AKM. In any case, the wire stock was folded, and the rifle was configured to be fired from the hip. It wasn't the kind of thing a casual street drunk carried.

And it was the kind of thing that justified the Executioner's move to take the guy out, without any inquiry about who he was and what he was doing.

The Ingram would have dropped him in an instant, with so little noise that the guys across the street wouldn't have noticed. On the other hand . . . maybe not. Even the silenced Beretta—if he'd had it with him—might have been heard by men on the roof across the street.

The warrior pulled out his Bali-Song.

A sentry was usually at a disadvantage. He was bored, he had to stay in one place, or at least in one

area, and often as not—as was the case with this one—
he couldn't position himself where he had an open
view of all approaches.

This one's duty was to focus his attention away from
the street, back into the passage he was supposed to be
guarding. But how long could a man stand, staring
fixedly into the darkness between a house and a
building? This one stood shifting from one foot to the
other, looking across the street most of the time, occasionally turning and peering into the passage.

Bolan, on the other hand, knew where to fix his attention, wasn't bored and could move when he chose.

He watched. The man wasn't predictable. You
couldn't time him. He glanced around at irregular intervals, but his interest was more on the building
across the street than on this dark, littered passageway. He shuffled his feet, flexed his shoulders.

And the Executioner, like a stalking tiger, moved
closer.

The sentry wore an ill-trimmed beard, the kind of
straggly whiskers young men not old enough to grow
full beards sometimes allowed to cover their faces. He
chewed gum, fiddled with his gun, apparently flick-
ing the safety on and off.

The guy peered into the darkness. Bolan was
crouched in a shadow, motionless, ready. The sentry
raised the muzzle of the rifle, threatening the darkness as if he could frighten away someone he couldn't
see, then swung around again and faced the street.

Bolan moved ten feet closer.

The man turned quickly and held the rifle on the
passageway. Maybe he'd heard Bolan move. Maybe he

imagined it. He swung the muzzle back and forth, then moved a pace into the passage. He kept the rifle pointed ahead, his finger on the trigger.

He swung to his left, shoving the muzzle toward the wall on the left. Bolan, on the right, could have taken him then, but the gunner would have squeezed off a roaring burst, alerting the Brigada. Bolan waited.

The man turned back toward the street again. For a moment he took his finger off the trigger as he used his right hand to wipe sweat from his brow.

Bolan moved. Throwing his left arm around the man's chest to pin his arms, he drew the Bali-Song across his throat. The sentry stiffened, then sagged. The AKM dropped from his left hand.

The Executioner dragged him backward into the passageway and dropped him to the ground.

The warehouse was less than fifty yards across the street. Bolan retrieved the Armbrust he'd left lying on the ground and checked the sights. They were as he had set them: ready to aim at fifty yards. He knelt and raised the tube launcher.

The target he'd selected was one of the cars he'd decided were filled with explosives. One of them was peculiarly close to the north wall of the warehouse—that is, on the back wall, away from the street where the loading door opened. He raised the Armbrust and took careful aim, then fired.

The missile launcher barked like a pistol. A storm of plastic flakes flew out the rear end, counteracting the recoil from the missile exiting the front so that Bolan wasn't jerked or shaken. Hiders concealed the flash at both ends.

The range was so short that the explosion seemed simultaneous with the launch. The car had been, as Bolan figured, loaded with high explosives. An eruption of brilliant yellow fire roared up where the car had been. The shock wave threw other vehicles away from their wires, but one more exploded from the shock and fire of the initial explosion, almost starting a chain reaction of explosions. Ragged shreds of sheet steel were all but invisible, rising on the boiling upheaval of fire.

For a moment fire enveloped the rear wall of the warehouse. When it subsided into smoke and small red flames, the concrete wall stood revealed—collapsed, leaving a huge entryway into the fort the Brigada Popular had built into this old auto agency.

Before Bolan moved to the second element of his assault he spotted enemy gunners inside the warehouse, directing a hail of fire through the gap toward the assault they expected from that side.

The warrior sprinted back to where Ramona and Alvarado waited, guarding the two remaining Armbrust launchers and watching for reinforcements from the nearby streets. He tossed his empty tube to the young man and grabbed another launcher.

Again the range was short. He took aim on the steel double doors through which he'd seen the liquor truck leave that afternoon. He fired. As expected, the armor-piercing missile penetrated one of the doors, leaving only a small hole but detonating inside with a tremendous explosion.

He picked up the third Armbrust, firing, this time, at the concrete wall to the right of the double doors.

The missile broke into the concrete as it had burst through the steel; but concrete was a substance it hadn't been designed to penetrate, and halfway through it went off with all the force of its two-pound charge of explosives and blew a five-foot-wide hole in the wall.

"Stay here!" Bolan yelled. "Protect my back!"

He sprinted across the street, SMG at the hip and ready. The chaos inside hadn't panicked the thoroughly trained men of the Brigada Popular. When the Executioner reached the breach in the wall, he saw that some of them had turned away from the hole at the rear of the building and were redeploying to face a threat from the front.

He let loose a burst of .45-caliber rounds through the hole in the wall. It chopped down two or three defenders, but another three or four fell back and took cover. When he reached the hole in the wall, he was faced with a storm of slugs chipping the edges of the concrete. He fired two bursts into the warehouse, but for a moment he was stopped.

The lights still burned on the ceiling inside. He could see something of the damage the Armbrust missile had done when it blew through the steel door. At least a hundred cases of liquor had been penetrated, and gallons of spirits were pouring onto the floor.

A blast sounded on the street. Reserves.

There were two carloads of them, one vehicle a convertible. They'd begun to fire on him as soon as they'd turned into the street, the guys in the convertible standing and blasting when they spotted the warrior in the light from inside the warehouse.

But Bolan's cubano companions saw the situation, too. Two angry bursts of 9 mm slugs from two mini-Uzis chopped the front of the convertible into a tangle of shredded steel. The vehicle careened to the curb and stopped.

The terrorists in the second car tried to speed through the street, firing on Bolan as they passed, but he swung the Ingram around and hit them with a burst of heavy slugs at the same instant gunfire from the two mini-Uzis jolted that car.

Six men, maybe eight, jumped from the two cars—straight into a hurricane of fire and steel pellets from one of the two grenades. Three fell. The driver of the convertible sat silently behind the wheel, his mouth and eyes wide open as if stunned by surprise.

Two men crouched in the street, rifles up and ready, looking for their target. But Bolan was no longer a silhouette against the light from inside the warehouse. He'd moved a pace back. As they searched for him, swinging their muzzles back and forth, he cut them down with two quick bursts from the Ingram.

One man ran, the other staggering along the side of the convertible, firing wildly into the air until he dropped to his knees and sprawled onto the pavement.

Bolan turned and fired a burst into the hole in the warehouse wall to keep back the gunmen inside. Then a new sound joined those of the raging battle—the wailing of sirens. The police were coming.

Ramona raced across the street and was beside him in seconds. Without a word she handed Bolan an-